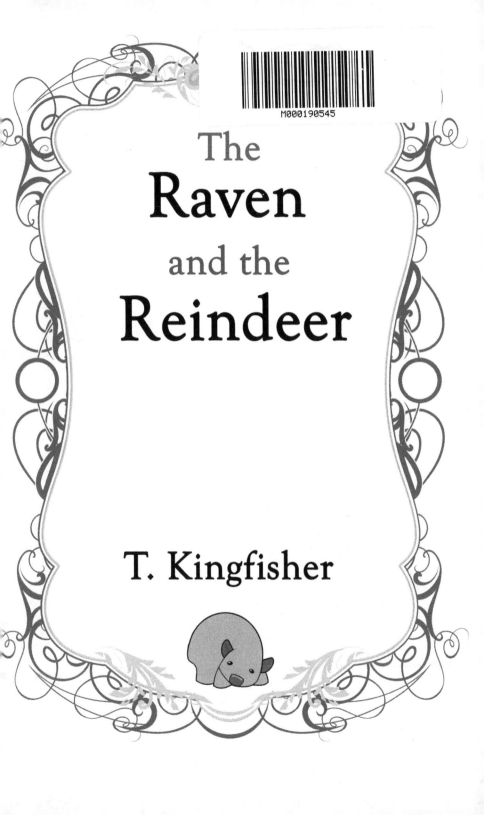

The
Raven
and the
Reindeer

T. Kingfisher

The Raven & The Reindeer

by T. Kingfisher

Argyll Productions
Dallas, Texas

The Raven & The Reindeer
Production copyright Argyll Productions © 2017

This is a work of fiction. Any resemblence to persons, places, plants,
poets, events, or actual historical personages, living, dead, or trapped in
a hellish afterlife is purely coincidental.

Published by Argyll Productions
Dallas, Texas
www.argyllproductions.com

ISBN 978-1-61450-583-9

First Edition Trade Paperback July 2017

Typeset in Adobe Garamond Pro and Goudy Old Style.

For Tina,
companion on many
adventures, who needed a
book with a bird
in it

Chapter One

Once upon a time, there was a boy born with frost in his eyes and frost in his heart.

There are a hundred stories about why this happens. Some of them are close to true. Most of them are merely there to absolve the rest of us of blame.

It happens. Sometimes it's no one's fault.

This boy was named Kay. His eyes were blue when he was born, pale as a winter sky. The frost glittered in them, in little flecks of silver around the pupil.

"What lovely eyes!" his grandmother said, rocking the baby on her knee. "He'll be a devil, with eyes like that."

"Lots of babies have blue eyes," said her best friend, who was knitting baby clothes. "They mostly grow out of it."

His grandmother clucked her tongue. "You won't say that when your grandbaby's born."

"I will, too."

"You would, wouldn't you?" Kay's grandmother laughed at that, and her friend smiled. "They'll be great friends, our grandbabies."

"If they don't grow out of that, too."

"Oh, *you*..." Something displeased Kay and he screwed up his face and squalled. "There. Your eyes *will* stay blue. Don't listen to that old sourpuss."

The old sourpuss in question only laughed.

The granddaughter was born a few days later, and her eyes were brown. They named her Gerta. She was chubby and good-natured and slept easily through the night.

Kay grew up tall and slim and his eyes stayed pale blue with a ring around them, like the eyes of a sled dog. His grandmother had been right about that.

Whether or not she was right in her other prediction was an open question.

Gerta would have said that Kay was her best and truest friend, that they could tell each other anything and they would take on the world together.

Kay would have said Gerta was the neighbor girl. "She's all right. I guess."

In fact, he did say this, on a number of occasions.

There are not many stories about this sort of thing. There ought to be more. Perhaps if there were, the Gertas of the world would learn to recognize it.

Perhaps not. It is hard to see a story when you are standing in the middle of it.

But if Kay had a sled-dog's eyes, Gerta had a dog's loyalty. It did not matter that he ignored her sometimes, or said "It's just the neighbor girl" to the other boys in the town. Those boys did not know what Gerta knew.

When it was cold (and it was often cold) when the snow was piled four feet deep under the eaves (and sometimes higher) then Kay would open the window in his family's garret and Gerta would open the window in hers. They were separated by less than three feet, and there was a little bit of a bridge between them, where Gerta's mother had set up a windowbox.

Then one or the other would step across the gap and into the other one's home. On cold days, the stove would be on and there would usually be something delicious on it—lingonberry juice or mulled cider or a plate of gingerbread.

The two of them would play together for hours as children. They were not much alike. Kay liked puzzles with pieces that you could fit together, and Gerta liked making up stories of heroes and gods and monsters. Gerta was only taller than Kay for three glorious months, when she got her growth spurt and he didn't. Then Kay shot up past her and Gerta never got any taller.

"That's just the way it is," her grandmother said. "We're short, sturdy people. Keeps us below the level of the wind."

"I'd rather be tall and beautiful," said Gerta.

"If wishes were fishes, we'd have herring for dinner."

"We're going to have pickled herring *anyway,*" said Gerta.

"Well, then who knows?" Her grandmother winked at her. "Perhaps there's some point to wishing after all."

As they got older, the children would talk—or Gerta would talk and Kay would comment occasionally, his slow sentences falling quiet as snowflakes.

"Sometimes I think that snow could be alive," he said once. "Like a hive of bees."

"I always think of feathers," said Gerta. "Like what if a snow goose flew over us and all the down shook out of its feathers?"

"It would have to be a big goose."

"Or a whole flock of them," Gerta agreed. "A whole flock of geese over the town, flapping their wings, and that's why it's windy too!"

Kay smiled faintly.

Another time he said, "I like the world better when it's snowed. You can't see all the ugly bits. It's all pure white."

He did not know that Gerta treasured these statements, saving them up and repeating them to herself at night. They were her great comfort. In summer, when he went around with the other boys and pretended to ignore her, she remembered his words.

She thought, *I bet he doesn't say things like that to the other boys. That's the part of himself he only shows to me. That's the important bit.*

11

Which only goes to show that you can be both right and completely wrong, all at the same time.

Chapter Two

The snow fell and melted and fell again. It fell for two days and then stopped. The sun came out and shone fiercely on the snow, enough to make you blind and dazzled.

The townspeople shoveled the walks and the horses were unhooked from wagons and hooked again to sleds.

Gerta stood at the window and gazed out through the frost-rimed panes. The glass squares were very small and her breath turned them white as she stood.

"He's gone out with his friends," said Gerta's grandmother. She was older now, but still knitting clothes for her granddaughter.

"We spent two days talking," said Gerta.

"Then you're probably sick of him by now."

Gerta shook her head. They had worked on a puzzle for a number of hours, and when they finished it at last, they had gone to get tea and Kay had kissed her behind the stove. It was a new experience and it made her feel strange and squashy. She'd expected...

Well, she wasn't sure what she expected.

His lips had been cool and a bit dry. She wasn't sure if she was supposed to push back with her lips or move her head or just stand there and have it happen.

She was in love with Kay, of course, always had been, so his kiss should have made her feel blissful and alive. She should have woken up from her ordinary life the way a fairy tale princess wakes from an enchanted sleep.

She probably shouldn't have been wondering what she was supposed to do with her lips.

I must have done it wrong. Maybe I was supposed to do something else.

If he'd do it again, maybe I could figure out what I was supposed to do.

In order to kiss her again, Kay would have to be somewhere nearby, not out sledding with his friends. Gerta sighed.

"You should go out with other girls," said her grandmother.

"I don't like the other girls," said Gerta, scowling. "Besides, I'm not *like* them."

(Kay had told her once that she wasn't much like other girls. It was one of the phrases that she held very close, tucked up in the space beneath her breastbone.)

"In this very town," said her grandmother, "there are at least a dozen girls standing at windows right this very minute saying the exact same thing." She shook out her knitting.

Gerta scowled harder.

"I did the same thing when I was your age," said her grandmother. "I daresay I wasn't like other girls harder than anyone else ever was. I was so unlike other girls that I wasn't even like myself, except on Sundays."

Gerta felt the scowl turn up at the edges and pressed her lips resolutely down.

"Go out with some other boys, then," said her grandmother. "At least meet a few." Almost under her breath, she added "Make Kay sweat a little, for a change."

"I don't like any other boys."

"Yes, and he knows it, too." Her grandmother shook her head. "Wouldn't hurt to meet them. Girls not much older than you are getting married, and I'd hate to have you settle for the boy next door."

"It's not settling," said Gerta, quite shocked. "It's *Kay.*"

"Yes, yes." Her grandmother held up her knitting. "Bother! I'm out of this color yarn, and I did think I'd have enough to finish. You won't mind if your sock turns green at the top, will you, Gerta?"

"One half-green sock?"

"I guarantee none of the other girls will have a sock like it. 'That girl,' they will say, 'that girl is *not* like other girls. Just look at her socks!'"

Gerta tried to hold onto the scowl, but it melted.

"There's my child," said her grandmother, pleased. "Do you know, I might have enough yarn to finish it up after all?"

"That's all right," said Gerta. "I think I'd like one half-green sock."

Kay did not kiss her again. Gerta went from the extremes of joy to the depths of despair, often several times in the same day.

He kissed me. That means he loves me.

He hasn't kissed me again. That means I did it wrong.

When his dad made a stupid joke, Kay rolled his eyes and smiled at me. That means...that means...

In the old days, Gerta knew, people used to write questions on reindeer bones and throw them into bonfires. The way the bones cracked told you the answers.

I wish I had a bonfire. And a reindeer skeleton.

Hard luck for the reindeer, though. I'd want it to be a very old reindeer who died peacefully.

It occurred to her that she could simply ask Kay if he loved her.

I'd die. I'd just die. On the spot. Immediately.

"Are you feeling well, child?" asked her grandmother. "You've gone all flushed."

"I'm fine!" said Gerta. She snatched up her mittens and ran outside.

The center of town was full of horse-drawn sledges, but there was a very fine sledding hill just three streets away. The road was never shoveled because it was much too steep for horses, so everyone took their sleds there.

She saw Kay with his sled. He wasn't wearing mittens or a hat, but he didn't look cold. His friends were more heavily wrapped.

Gerta felt self-conscious. It was all very well to be short and sturdy, but when she was bundled up in coats, she felt wider than she was tall.

"Hey, Gerta," said one of the boys, pulling his scarf down so he could talk. He was a shorter boy with dark, curly hair.

Kay looked her over coolly and dipped his head once.

"You want to have a go at the hill?" asked the curly-haired boy. "You can use my sled."

"Well…" said Gerta. She was hoping Kay would offer her his sled.

Kay picked up his sled instead. "I'm done," he announced to no one in particular. "I'm going home."

"I'll come with you," said Gerta. "Thanks, though."

The curly-haired boy shrugged. "Come back if you change your mind."

They walked home together. Gerta had to stretch her legs to keep up.

"What's your friend's name?" she asked. "He seemed nice."

"Bran." Kay's jaw was set. He looked angry. Gerta wondered if she'd done something wrong.

I shouldn't have said he seemed nice. He probably thinks I like Bran more than him. Oh that was a stupid thing to say.

They walked three blocks, while Gerta tried to think of something to say that would let him know that she liked him best of all.

"I wish it would snow again," said Kay abruptly.

"Oh, me too!" said Gerta, who would have agreed to anything at this point.

"A really big storm," said Kay. "A blizzard."

Gerta was less sure about this. "Why a blizzard?"

"So everything is covered," said Kay. "Everything's white. And crisp. And when you walk on the snow, it's like you're the only person in the world."

"It sounds beautiful."

"You could walk for miles," said Kay, "and listen to the wind."

"Wouldn't it be cold?"

"Yes. That's the point."

"Oh."

They kept walking. Gerta felt as if she were trudging. The snow was loose and wet and every footstep sank deep.

She glanced at Kay. "Aren't you cold right now, though? You don't have a hat."

"I never get cold," said Kay.

Chapter Three

Kay got his wish. The snow came down that night like the end of the world. Wind howled under the eaves and frost chewed on the edges of the windows. And the snow fell and fell and fell.

"A hundred-year storm," said Gerta's grandmother. "The Snow Queen rides tonight."

Gerta and Kay had been standing at the window, watching the snow fall. Gerta's nose was nearly frozen off, but Kay was there and she was very happy.

"Who's the Snow Queen?" asked Kay.

"The queen of all this," said Gerta's grandmother. "The mistress of ice. She has a palace as far north as north. She rides in a sleigh made of ice and pulled by great white bears who used to be men." (Gerta's grandmother knew how a story ought to be told, even if she wasn't always sure how much yarn went into a sock.)

Kay raised an eyebrow and sipped his hot cider.

"How did they turn into bears?" asked Gerta.

"The Snow Queen enchanted them," said her grandmother. "She's Circe's cold cousin, always turning men into other beasts. Not pigs, though. She likes bears and seals and wolves and all the creatures of ice."

"Sounds rotten of her," said Gerta.

"Oh, I daresay she had her reasons," said her grandmother, who could think of a few men that would have been much improved by spending time as an enchanted seal.

"What does she look like?" asked Kay dreamily.

"White as white," said Gerta's grandmother. "She wears the furs of white foxes and her sleigh is cut from birch trees." She took a sip of her cider. "The snow follows her wherever she goes. When she's in a temper, she brings down ice storms and the trees fall down like matchsticks."

"Why would she do that?" asked Gerta.

Her grandmother shrugged. "She's the Snow Queen. It's what she does."

She got up to mull more cider. Kay and Gerta stood at the window, watching the snow whirl down.

They were shoulder to shoulder in the window. Gerta leaned on Kay a little, and he leaned back.

She felt a rush of relief. *He isn't still angry with me about this morning. If he was angry with me at all…*

She wondered if he would kiss her again. Maybe this time she could figure out what she was supposed to do with her lips.

But he didn't, and the minutes stretched out and her grandmother came back into the room with more cider, bustling back and forth between the counter and the stove.

Gerta stifled a sigh. She had lived next door to Kay her entire life, and sometimes he was cold and sometimes he was warm. There never seemed to be any pattern to it. He might spend an entire day playing adventures with her, or letting her help with a puzzle, and then the next day he'd shrug one shoulder when she came near and refuse to meet her eyes.

Oh well. He kissed me once. He knows I'm here, and nearly grown up. And he doesn't have an understanding with any other girl, because he would have told me.

Her lips twisted, looking out at the snow. She could be sure of this. It would not have occurred to Kay that telling her about another girl would make her jealous.

That's 'cos we're best friends. And best friends tell each other everything.

She slid a glance at Kay. His dark eyelashes framed his pale blue eyes, as he drank in the blowing snow. Whatever he was thinking, he kept it to himself.

That night Gerta slept in her trundlebed near the stove. She curled up under the green-patched quilt and there she dreamed.

She dreamed that the snow had stopped and the moonlight glowed through the window. Some sound had roused her attention—a high thin chiming, like bridle bells.

I could get up.

It's so warm here. It'll be cold by the window.

She looked up into the shadows of the ceiling. The rafters were hung with baskets. Her grandmother baked flat, hard loaves of bread and strung them on wooden poles to keep them. They were delicious when crumbled up and soaked in the juices of rabbit or chicken or deer.

The sound came again. *Tingatingatinga-ting-ting-ting.*

She pushed off her quilt and walked to the window.

Everything was white and blue and silver. The walls of the building across the alley were dark smears, crowned with thick white cliffs of snow.

Tingatingatingatinga…

Down the rooftop came a white sleigh, cut from shining birch wood. Bells rang merrily along the traces.

There is a sleigh on the roof, Gerda thought, and then, *Ah. I am dreaming.*

Because she was dreaming, she did not question that the sleigh was pulled by snow-white otters. They slipped and slithered down the slant of the roof, sliding over each other, a river of white fur and black eyes and arched white whiskers. Gerda kept expecting the traces to get tangled, but somehow the sled kept moving forward.

At the edge of the roof, the sleigh stopped. The otters pulled up, chuckling and chirping to each other in liquid voices. They were larger than any otters that Gerda had ever seen. They had pale blue bridles with silver bells and their webbed feet moved across the snow like snowshoes.

Gerta was so fascinated by the otters that she hadn't looked at the sled at all. She tore her eyes away from them with reluctance.

It was a relatively small sleigh, only large enough for one or two people. *Of course,* thought Gerta, *otters probably can't pull very much weight, not like horses or reindeer...*

The runners were ivory, carved in the shape of leaping seals. The trim was ice blue and matched the bridles.

Seated in the sleigh was a woman.

Gerta, who had been highly delighted by the sleigh and the otters, felt the first chill.

The woman was very tall and very slim. Her face was as angular as a fox and her hair was white, yet somehow she did not look old. She sat in the sled with her hands on the reins and looked around, and the world seemed to change as she gazed down at it.

The buildings and the streets became small and shabby. The town looked old and grimy. Gerta, who loved her town, caught her breath at the injustice of it, because nothing about the town *had* changed, it was only that the woman in the sleigh was so far above it all.

Only the snow remained clean and white, still glowing in the moonlight. The woman in the sleigh did not look at the moon, and some small, wise part of Gerta thought, *I bet she can't. It doesn't change if you look at it. No matter how pale and pure and perfect you are, the moon is even more perfect.*

Gerta, who was short and sturdy and turned pink when she hurried, felt her hands clench into fists.

I wish I would wake up. The otters were wonderful but I don't want to see the rest of this.

The Snow Queen—*surely it must be the Snow Queen, surely it could be no one else*—stepped out of the sleigh. She wore white deerskin boots, exquisitely small, and left no track upon the snow.

Gerta jerked back, suddenly afraid that the Snow Queen would see her.

She can't touch me. If she touches me, something bad will happen.

For a moment, she thought that she was safe. The woman would leave. The dream would end and in the morning perhaps all she would remember would be the otters.

Then a pale oval appeared at the other window, directly across from Gerta.

It was Kay.

No! Gerta wanted to yell. *No, go back inside, don't let her see you!*

But this was a dream and dreams are the sisters of nightmares. She could not yell and her hands curled into useless fists on the window frame.

The Snow Queen walked to the edge of the roof and smiled down at Kay.

Kay's mouth fell open.

For a long moment, they looked at each other. Their eyes, Gerta saw, were the same color.

The Snow Queen crooked her finger, curled it back.

No! Kay, no, run away! If she touches you—!

She did not quite know what would happen, only that it would be terrible.

Kay pushed the window open and began to climb out.

The iron railings between the two windows, the highway on which Kay and Gerta moved back and forth, was slick with ice. Gerta covered her mouth with her hands, afraid that he might fall—

—it's better if he falls, the snow is thick, he'll probably live, if she touches him he'll die or worse—

The Snow Queen reached down and took his hand.

Kay gasped. Even through the glass, Gerta could hear it. He gasped and for a single heartbeat, his eyes glowed like ice in the moonlight.

The Snow Queen's bones were fine and delicate, but her strength was enormous. She pulled him onto the rooftop and helped him into her sled.

Gerta couldn't help it. She slapped a hand against the cold glass. "Kay!" she cried. Her voice seemed to come from very far away.

He did not look around. He settled himself in the sled, under a blanket trimmed with white fox-fur.

The Snow Queen turned and looked down at Gerta.

Gerta jerked back as if she'd been lashed with a whip.

The Snow Queen's gaze was no kinder to her than it was to the town around them. Gerta felt young and weak and disgustingly mortal. She was a stinking, bleating creature, a heifer-calf with muck tangled in her tail. She did not deserve to share the same air with the magnificent Snow Queen.

Her back wanted to bow and her legs wanted to buckle. She wanted to grovel and apologize for existing. She wanted to hide her eyes and crawl away.

I can't—I can't—she's got Kay—I've got to stop her, but she's so much better *than me—*

And then, as if from a very great distance, she thought, *Grandmother wouldn't crawl.*

Gerta sank down to her knees under the window…but she did not look away from the Snow Queen's eyes.

The Queen reared back a little, like a great swan arching her neck. She turned back toward Kay.

Gerta gasped as if a stranglehold had suddenly been broken.

The Queen stepped into the sleigh, bent down, and kissed Kay on the cheek.

She slapped the reins and the otters rose up, cheerful and chiming. The sleigh began to move down the edge of the rooftop.

"No," whispered Gerta. Her throat was hoarse, as if she had been screaming. A whisper was all she could manage. "No!"

The Snow Queen looked over at her.

She smiled.

It was a nasty, cold smile, but at the same time, it was more human than any expression Gerta had seen on the Snow Queen's face. It was a smile that said *I have something you want, and it's mine now, and you'll never get it back.*

Kay gazed forward and never looked behind him.

The otters leapt from the roof and the sleigh followed. It would have been an enormous drop, but it did not occur to Gerta to worry. They would ride a snow flurry down, or a sheet of icicles. The Snow Queen would not be stopped by anything so foolish as a three-story building.

They were gone.

The only tracks on the rooftop were the holes left by Kay's feet, and they filled up with snow so fast that they might as well not have been there at all.

Gerta stayed at the window until her teeth chattered, but there was no point. She knew there was no point.

She crept to the trundle bed and pulled the quilt over her head.

It was a dream, thought Gerta forlornly. *It was all a dream. I'll wake up and I won't remember it very well at all and we'll laugh about it. I hope I remember the otters, but I'd like to forget her.*

In the morning, Kay was gone.

Chapter Four

There is a great deal that goes on when someone goes missing, and none of it is good. It is a tiresome sort of panic, because there is no end to it. It goes on and on and on until you are hollowed out and empty and still there is no end.

First the families told each other that Kay was fine, that he had just stepped out to go sledding. It was a bit odd that he had left a puzzle half-done like that, but boys were odd sometimes.

Then they told each other that he had gotten lost but would turn up shortly. They would laugh about how foolish they were being.

Then they told each other that he was clearly lost in the snow but he was a smart lad and would dig down where he was and be safe.

Eventually the snow melted and the sun shone down and thaw came and went and they stopped telling each other anything at all.

Through all those long weeks, Gerta felt as if she was standing a little apart from everyone else. It was as if her dream had raised a wall of ice and the world was on the far side of it.

If *it was a dream.*

It can't have been a dream.

It must have been a dream.

I know what I saw.

He wouldn't have gone out in a blizzard. He isn't a fool.

She lived the last moments of the dream a thousand times, seeing Kay look up, his lips parted, looking at the strange cold woman with an expression of lust and worship. The expression made her stomach clench like a fist.

I want it to be a dream because I don't want him to look at anyone else like that.

I want it to be true because I don't want him to be dead!

When she put it like that, there was no choice at all.

The woman had been so beautiful. Gerta's heart ached for how beautiful she had been. She wanted to be able to turn to someone and say, "Did you see that?"

But no one else had seen her. Perhaps there had been no one else awake to see.

And the wall of ice stood between Gerta and the rest of the world, and she could not reach through it to say, "He isn't dead. I saw him leaving in a dream."

Gerta's grandmother made hot tea in endless amounts, melting snow into water and throwing handfuls of herbs into it. The tea was the only thing that Kay's grandmother would drink.

"My sweet little boy," whispered Kay's grandmother, her voice gone hoarse with weeping. "My sweet boy. Where did he go?"

"You'll do no good following him into the next world," said Gerta's grandmother bluntly. "Eat some soup."

Gerta silently appeared with soup in a mug and the old woman drank it. She had become old, it seemed, in the time since the spring thaw.

When she slept at last, her hair was a silver fan over the pillow. Gerta's grandmother stroked it, her face lined and weary. In the distance, they could hear water dripping from the eaves, *drip drip drip* as the ice melted away.

Perhaps it was the thaw that made the first crack in the wall of ice around Gerta. Perhaps it was the steam from the soup or the tears on the old woman's pillow.

"Grandmother?"

"Eh? Yes, child?"

"Is the Snow Queen real?" asked Gerta.

Her grandmother looked at her for a moment as if she could not understand the question. After a moment, she said "I suppose she's real enough. Stranger things have walked the earth and left stories behind them."

"I saw her," said Gerta. "The night Kay...that night. I saw a sleigh on the roof. There was a woman in it, all over white. I thought I was dreaming, but Kay's gone. He's not coming back. I think she has him."

Her grandmother made the sign to avert evil.

"Tell me about this woman."

Gerta tried, at great length. Her tongue stumbled on some of the descriptions—on how beautiful the woman was, and on the look on Kay's face. But parts of it she remembered clearly, like how the sleigh had looked and the way the runners had been a hundred carved ivory seals, slithering and sliding over top of one another.

Her grandmother drew in a sharp breath at that, for she had heard such things before, and she was certain that she had never mentioned them aloud.

After a long time, she said, "You've never lied, Gerta, even when you were little and trying to get out of trouble. Even when you were trying to cover up for Kay, you'd just stand there, stubborn as a little stone, and not say anything. If you say you saw the Snow Queen, I'll not disbelieve you now."

"As far north as north," said Gerta. She took a deep breath and let it out. She was aware that what she was doing was quite unspeakably mad. "I have to go after him."

Her grandmother closed her eyes. After a moment, she said, "I should tell you not to go. I should tell you one child lost is enough."

"But you won't," said Gerta.

"But I won't." She looked back at her oldest and dearest friend, asleep on the couch with the lines of age and grief like fissures in her skin. "I'm an old fool. I told you and Kay about the Snow

Queen. I should have known he'd take it to heart. There always was a spot of ice in him."

"You couldn't know—" said Gerta.

"I should have known. Things come when they're called." She scrubbed her hands over her own face. "If I lose you, it's no more than I deserve."

"I'll be careful," said Gerta. "You won't lose me. I'll just go north a little way and ask if anyone's seen him."

"Yes." Her grandmother began hurrying around the room. "Take some food. I don't want you starving."

Gerta slung her pack over her back. "I will. Is there anything else I can do, Grandmother? Against the Snow Queen?"

The old woman shook her head. "In all the old stories, the only thing that ever won was love. And occasionally a good sharp knife."

"I'll take the kitchen knife with me, then," said Gerta.

"Mind that you do. And wear your boots." She kissed her granddaughter on the forehead. "An old woman's grace go with you, child."

Gerta went.

Chapter Five

Spring had advanced far enough that it only sometimes froze at night, but it could not be said that it was warm. The roads were muddy. Gerta's boots squelched as she walked.

For the first few hours, her heart was light. She was going somewhere. She was *doing* something. She would get Kay back.

But as the evening started to fall, so did her spirits. Her calves ached from sliding back and forth in the mud. Her toes were very cold.

I can't have come very far, not really. But I've been walking for hours. And where am I going to sleep?

In stories, the heroines were resourceful and cheerful and determined. Gerta had hoped to be all these things, but the sun was sinking behind the trees and she was feeling less and less resourceful. Cheerful was right out.

Shouldn't there be a farmhouse somewhere? I could trade chores for a place to sleep... but that only works if there's a farmhouse somewhere...

She was, in fact, in the woods. They were not dark or scary or twisted woods, but they were deep and full of sounds. Insects went *skreek skreek* and frogs went *hnaaaaagh* and an owl went *Eeeeaaaagahahahah!* and Gerta nearly jumped out of her skin.

She squelched down the road in a hurry, her heart pounding. Even knowing that it was an owl didn't help.

I should stop. I can hardly see. I could wander off a cliff.

Oh yes. Because there are lots and lots of cliffs in the middle of well-travelled wagon roads...

She kept walking.

A fallen log by the side of the road offered a refuge. She sat down on it and sighed.

I suppose I could just sit here all night…

She knew that it wasn't cold enough to actually freeze to death. But the log was cold and damp and her backside got cold and damp and Gerta felt thoroughly miserable.

If I'm going to feel awful anyway, I might as well keep walking. At least I'll get closer to Kay.

She got up. The ground sucked at her boots as she slogged back onto the road.

An hour or so passed. Probably. She couldn't see the moon through the trees. The thought that it might only have been a few minutes was so discouraging that she tried not to think about it.

She was cold and she was tired. She had been sweating from exertion, so now her skin felt soggy. There was definitely a blister coming up on her heel.

It's for Kay, she told herself. *It's all worth it for Kay.*

Kay seemed very far away.

I will tell him all about this. He'll be very impressed. He'll say, "Oh, Gerta, how you've suffered for me…"

She engaged in this fantasy for a few moments, and then sighed. She was fundamentally honest, even with herself. Kay would look at her and say "You walked through the woods and it was cold? *That's* your great suffering?"

"It was scary," she would say. "And I had a blister."

Gerta could actually hear in her head how "I had a blister" would hang in the air between them. She flushed a little, at the sheer stupidity of the thing she hadn't actually said yet.

She kept walking. She tried to swing her right foot so that the heel wouldn't rub. It was only partially successful.

The road began to go uphill. Gerta wanted to cry and hated herself for it, because all she was doing was walking down a muddy road in the dark. You didn't get to cry about just walking down a road.

The Snow Queen could be days and days north of here. She probably is days and days north of here. I'll have to walk the whole way, and there won't be farmhouses for most of it. I'll have to sleep in the woods. And make camp. And build fires.

She took a deep breath. She knew how to build a fire in a stove. Presumably it wasn't that much different from building a fire on the ground. Making camp…well…that was something else again.

Her grandmother had taught her any number of things, like embroidery and spinning and plain sewing and some basic knitting. She had started to teach her how to use the great loom that stood in the corner, so that someday Gerta could earn her living as a weaver, if she didn't marry, or if she outlived her husband as her grandmother had done. And Gerta could cook on a stove and clean nearly anything. All good, useful skills. She'd make someone a fine wife some day. Everybody said so.

Making someone a fine wife had not included learning how to sleep in the woods without freezing or getting soaked. This struck Gerta as an enormous and unexpected gap in her education.

This is stupid. This isn't suffering. I don't get to feel bad about this.

Feeling bad about feeling bad was not significantly better than feeling bad in the first place. Gerta sighed again.

I will learn how to make a camp. I will learn how to sleep in the woods. I will find someone to teach me or I will figure it out myself.

People do it all the time. I'm not stupid, even if I'm not as smart as Kay. If I can take apart a stove, I can do this.

She squared her shoulders and went on.

Her newfound determination bought her a few more hours. The hill crested and going downhill helped.

She tried not to think about how long she had been walking.

I'll sing. It'll be easier if I sing a song.

She tried to think of one, and for some reason all that came to her was a hymn which she'd never even liked very much.

"The rose in the valley is blooming so sweet," she sang, "and angels descend there the children to greet."

Her voice died away. There were no roses here, and if there were angels, they were staying well hidden.

Eventually the world was no longer black but a seeping brownish-grey. Each twig was outlined with cold light.

Gerta did not really notice that it was dawn. She had moved from thinking too much to a place where she was no longer thinking at all. The pain on her heel had been absorbed by a general pain in her feet and her back and her hips and her shoulders.

She also did not notice that the trees were getting thinner or that the pines had given way to scruffy brambles with green buds on them. All she saw was the road.

It was not until she emerged from the woods completely that she stopped. Morning light broke over her like a wave.

"What...?" she said aloud, looking up, as if someone had spoken her name.

There was a farmhouse in the distance.

It stood by the side of a stream. The whitewashed sides sparkled. Gardens ran around it on three sides, dotted with green as the spring plants emerged.

Gerta stared at it for a long time, then lurched toward it.

Chores, she thought fixedly. *I must do chores. You go to the farmhouse and ask to do chores and they give you a place to sleep. In the barn, I think.*

She had never slept in a barn in her life. Presumably there was straw. You could sleep on straw, if you didn't mind being jabbed by a thousand individual pointy bits.

At the moment, Gerta would have slept on a bed of thorns if it meant that she could lie down.

The door was bright turquoise, painted with small white roses. She limped up the steps and stared at it stupidly for a moment.

Do I go in?

No. I knock. Knocking is a thing people do.

She knocked.

Footsteps sounded. A door banged. A moment later, the front door opened, and a middle-aged woman stood in the doorway. She had on a very extraordinary hat, covered in even more painted flowers.

"Yes?" she said, wiping her hands on her apron. "May I help you?"

Gerta blinked at her in surprise. Somehow, groggy with cold and walking, the fact that she would have to talk to another person had not really occurred to her.

Oh. Yes. There would be someone, wouldn't there?

Of course there would be a person. *Ask at the farmhouse* did not mean that you addressed your questions to the front porch. She had not thought it through.

I have been stupid. Kay would laugh at me. She flushed a little and lifted her chin and realized that she had been standing there staring at the woman for nearly half a minute.

"I'm sorry," said Gerta. "I'm...I'm sorry. I've been walking. Uh." She raised a hand and pushed the hair out of her face. Her cheeks felt very cold and she wondered when she had stopped being able to feel them.

The woman's face softened. "Oh, my dear," she said. "Have you been walking long?"

"All night," said Gerta. She thought for a moment. There was something important—"Chores. I'm supposed to do chores for you and ask for a place to sleep. Please, ma'am, if you don't mind."

Well, it wasn't elegant, but she seemed to have gotten all the right words out, even if they weren't in quite the right order.

The woman smiled. "Of course," she said. "I have plenty of chores you can do. But first come and get warm and rest."

This sounded wonderful to Gerta.

She went inside the house. The turquoise door painted with roses closed behind her, and the lock went *snick*.

There was a fire on the hearth. The woman in the flower hat led her to a chair in front of the fire. "My name is Helga," she said. "Please, get warm and make yourself comfortable."

Gerta sank into the chair. It was very soft and overstuffed and she was not sure that she would be able to get out of it again, but that was all right.

"Why did you walk all night?" asked Helga, bringing her a cup of something hot. The steam smelled of herbs.

"I have to find Kay," said Gerta. "My friend. The Snow Queen took him."

She looked up at Helga through the steam and it seemed that the woman was frowning. But by the time she had finished the hot drink (was it tea? She couldn't tell.), Helga was smiling again. "Rest," she suggested. "Warm your feet."

Gerta bent down to untie her shoes. She remembered getting the right one off, and had just started on the left when sleep crept up and hit her.

Chapter Six

Gerta woke in bed.

She did not feel any disorientation, although she wasn't sure where she was. The ceiling was high and whitewashed. She was lying in a small, snug trundle bed with a bright red quilt covered in roses. Her shoes were tucked down by the foot.

She got up, and the woman in the painted hat came to the door, smiling. *Helga. Her name was Helga.*

"Come and eat breakfast," said Helga.

"I'm supposed to do chores for you," said Gerta, remembering.

"You can weed the garden," said Helga. "*After* breakfast."

Breakfast was large. So was the garden. Chickweed, which loved a cold spring, overran the corners of the vegetable beds and formed green hillocks under the bare rosebushes.

Gerta set to work, gouging out great damp handfuls and throwing them into a basket. There were springs when chickweed was the first green food available, when everyone in town ate chickweed salads three times a day to keep from getting winter sickness.

"Come and eat," said Helga, when Gerta had weeded half the garden.

Gerta wiped her hands on her apron. Her fingers smelled green.

After lunch, she had thought to move on, but there was still so much to weed in the garden. *Tomorrow,* she thought. *I will set out again tomorrow. Helga is living alone* (for there was no one else in the house) *and needs my help. I will go out tomorrow after Kay. One day will make no difference.*

She was not eager to start out again, in truth, especially not so late in the day. The open fields would be cold at night. If she set out in the morning, she could get farther, and perhaps find another house to stay at, or at least a haystack. Travelling all night was clearly a bad idea.

Tomorrow.

She dreamed that night of chickweed, which was a strange thing to dream about. Chickweed is a low, weedy little plant, not very distinguished. No one writes poetry comparing their lovers to chickweed (or if they do, the poems are rarely well received).

In her dreams, she stood in a field of it, and the plants grew over her feet, cool as well-water. Tiny white flowers spangled the field like stars.

"Have you seen Kay?" she asked sadly. "I must find him."

"*Ahhhh…*" whispered the flowers, and the sound went out around her in a circle, like a wind blowing. "*Ahhhh…who is Kay… we do not know…*"

"He is my friend," said Gerta. "The Snow Queen took him."

The chickweed shivered. Gerta knelt and ran her hand over the stems, and they rippled into water, reflective, as if she stood knee-deep in a green pool.

In the surface, she saw another garden, surrounded by high walls. A girl with dark skin knelt in that garden, cutting plants with a knife. She wore a red dress and her face was sad and angry.

Gerta was afraid to move, for fear of disturbing the scene before her.

The girl stood, turning her head back toward a doorway. The anger faded, became only sorrow and confusion. She went through the doorway. A hedgehog trundled across the garden path, looking for slugs.

The vision faded. The water was no longer water but plants again, a sea of cold-weather weeds.

"That wasn't Kay," said Gerta. "I don't know who it was. I'm sorry."

The chickweed sighed. *"Ahhh...."* and Gerta woke.

She was lying in a small, snug trundle bed with a bright red quilt covered in roses.

She got up, and Helga came to the door in her painted hat, smiling.

"Come and eat breakfast," said Helga.

"I'm supposed to do chores for you," said Gerta, trying to remember...something. A dream? Where had it gone?

"You can weed the garden," said Helga. "After breakfast."

The peas were coming up in the garden. Gerta spent the morning wrapping the twining stems up poles. Small white flowers gaped open, perfuming the air. Bees buzzed around them, climbing inside, drunk on the fragrance.

There were a great many peas. The morning was gone before she noticed. *Tomorrow,* she thought. *I will set out again tomorrow after Kay. One day will make no difference.*

Her dream that night was of twining peas, sweetly scented. She stood inside a bower, looking up at the vines from inside. They rustled and whispered to her in many voices. Bees climbed through the flowers, and the buzzing joined the whisper of leaves until it sounded almost like speech.

"I must find Kay," said Gerta. "Have you seen him...?"

"Who is Kay...Kay...Kay..." asked the plants, making their own echoes.

"He's my friend. The Snow Queen took him."

The bees buzzed angrily, for bees fear snow, but the peas laughed, because frost on their stems does not bother them. The movement of leaves formed a stream of outlines, in curling green threads—a girl, a goat, a monster, a spoon.

Gerta shook her head.

The threads twined together like a tapestry. She saw a boat on the ocean, a great beast under the water, an island. Someone stood in the prow of the boat. The drone of the bees became a roar of triumph.

"No," said Gerta. "No, I don't know who that is. I'm sorry."

The tapestry came apart, and Gerta woke.

She was lying in the trundlebed, with the red quilt. Her fingers moved over the embroidered roses and she smiled.

Helga came to the door, in her painted hat. "Come and have breakfast."

"I should work in the garden," said Gerta.

"After breakfast," said Helga.

The peas were nearly spent. She harvested the pods. The bees had moved on to the earliest roses, and Gerta was busy picking beetles and slugs off the roses until mid-afternoon. Then came a long evening of shelling peas.

It seemed, as she stared down at her hands, her thumb splitting open the pods and sliding the peas out into the bowl, that she was forgetting something. There was something she was supposed to do...something important...

"Is everything all right, my dear?" asked Helga.

"Fine," said Gerta slowly. "Fine. Is there something I am supposed to be doing? I can't seem to remember..."

"Just keep me company," said Helga, patting Gerta's knee. "I'm so glad to have you here, my dear. I was so lonely without you."

Tomorrow, Gerta thought. *I'll remember it tomorrow.*

When she lay down in the trundlebed that night, Helga brought her a cup of something hot. The steam smelled of herbs.

"Drink," Helga said. "You're looking tired."

"A long day weeding," said Gerta, and smiled. "I'm fine, truly."

But she drank the cup obediently, and laid back in bed, under the red quilt.

Her hands moved fitfully over the embroidered roses, and it was not until she jabbed herself on a thorn that she realized she was dreaming.

She put her finger in her mouth. The taste of blood bloomed on her tongue and she stood in a courtyard surrounded by sweet-scented roses. They were larger than the ones in Helga's garden, nearly as large as Gerta's head, and vines scrambled between them, covered in golden trumpet flowers. A fountain sprayed into a pond full of darting fish.

There was a boy in the courtyard. He was looking into the water, and as Gerta watched, he smiled, showing a wide gap in his front teeth.

"No," she whispered to the roses, "no, this isn't who I'm looking for." She could not quite remember who she was looking for, but this was certainly not him.

She came half-awake and turned over on her side, pulling the quilt up. She thought Helga was standing in the doorway, watching her, but turning her head seemed too much effort and she slept again, without dreams.

The days passed, and the spell on Gerta deepened. Helga was not a powerful witch, as such things are measured, but she did not need to be powerful for this. Gerta's desire to be useful was an open road down which nearly any magic could walk.

"It is for her own good," Helga whispered to herself, fiercely. "It is for her own good. She would never reach the Snow Queen. She would be set upon by bandits, wolves, bears, anyone at all. And if she *did* somehow reach the Snow Queen…"

She shuddered. The notion of Gerta, who was sturdy and cheerful and kind and quite desperately mortal standing up against that terrible icy power…

"She is safe here," said Helga. She rested her forehead against the windowpane, gazing out at the garden. "She is safe and she is not unhappy and I am glad of the company."

In the garden, the plants shivered. A rose dropped its petals, one by one, in rebuke.

"You don't have to like it," said Helga. "The important thing is that she's safe."

The plants did not like it. A witch's garden gains a sense of itself before long, drinking magic in with the mulch and the rain. They knew that Gerta was looking for someone and they knew by their roots that he was not down under the earth, down among the dead.

But to plants, most humans look alike, and so the dreams they sent Gerta ranged far afield, in distance and in time, based on some unknown vegetative logic.

From the grapevines came a vision of a girl a little older than she was, with dark amber skin and thick black curls. She wore a bright scarf and a half-dozen wood pigeons moved around her, cooing to one another. Gerta thought she had an interesting face, and would have liked to know her better.

The rowan tree at the end of the garden sent her a dream of a heron standing at the edge of a lake. A man approached in ragged finery, and the heron turned and bowed like a courtier to a king.

The apple tree, as autumn approached and the small green apples swelled on the stems, sent her dreams of a child with hair as white as bone and eyebrows that stood out like scars. Gerta could not tell if the child was male or female, but she knew that she was looking for someone else, and the dream of apple leaves dissolved.

She did not know what to make of the dream sent to her by the bindweed, of three white foxes having tea together, drinking from delicate lacquer teacups—and likely no human would have known *what* to think of the vision brought by the reeds, of golden fish speaking soberly to one another in a language made of fin-twitches and scale ripples.

None of the dreams held what she was looking for, and the spell grew thicker and more entrenched, and she did not think of leaving.

Chapter Seven

Gerta stood in the garden, pulling out the dead annuals. Frost had killed them down to their roots, and there was nothing left but to put them on the compost pile.

She stood and stretched. Her breath steamed in the air. The garden smelled of leaf mold and woodsmoke; a good smell, a harvest smell.

A wedge of geese flew overhead, honking. Gerta smiled up at them, and then a single snow flake caught her eye, and another, and another. "Snow!" she said, out loud. "Like down falling from a goose!"

Unbidden, the memory rose, of someone saying, *It would have to be a big goose.*

"Or a whole flock of them…" she said slowly, remembering the conversation, remembering it as clearly as if Kay was standing next to her and she was standing at the window.

Kay.

She shuddered suddenly, violently, as if she had sobbed. She did not know it, but it was the spell sundering.

Inside the house, Helga cried out.

Gerta turned, slowly, seeing the garden as if for the first time. The beds were bare, except for the last root vegetables still in the ground, under a layer of straw. It might almost have been early spring, but the geese had flown in the wrong direction, and oak and apple leaves lay strewn about the path. There were red hips on the rosebushes.

The snowflakes, barely a flurry, landed and melted almost at once.

"It's autumn," said Gerta. Horror stole over her. "It's autumn. I set out in spring. What has happened? How long—?"

Helga burst from the house. "Gerta!" she said. "Gerta, my dear, come inside—please, I can explain—"

Gerta backed away, shaking her head. "No," she said. "No! Stay away!"

Helga might not have stopped, but Gerta screamed—Gerta, who never screamed, who could not raise her voice without blushing—*"I said stay away!"*

The older woman halted. Her face trembled, all the parts of it, as if it might collapse. "Gerta..."

"How long have I been here?"

Helga held up her hands. The painted flowers on her hat shuddered. "Seven months," she admitted. "But Gerta—"

Gerta staggered and had to catch herself on a wooden trellis. It creaked under her weight.

"Seven months," she said. A snowflake swirled past her face and she stared at it. "Seven months."

"I couldn't let you go!" said Helga. "You would have died...the Snow Queen would have killed you...you've been safe here, haven't you? I've been protecting you!"

Gerta barely heard her. She wracked her mind for memories of the last few months and all she had were fragments. She remembered working in the garden and strange dreams. Surely it had only been a week or two, surely not more than that...

Seven months.

Her birthday had come and gone, nearly half a year ago. Gerta choked on a laugh or a sob. She was suddenly closer to eighteen than sixteen.

They've had the harvest feast back home. The sweetheart's dance. Kay would have asked me to dance, I'm sure of it, but he didn't because the Snow Queen took him, and I went after him, and I only got this far...

She was consumed with shame. Barely a day and a night down the road—fifteen miles from home? Twenty?—and she had been here seven months. Her grandmother undoubtedly thought she was dead.

Kay might be dead.

"It will be all right," said Helga anxiously. "Come inside—I promise—I'm sorry—"

"Stay away from me," said Gerta again. She backed toward the garden gate. "I have to find Kay."

"You can't leave now," said Helga. "It's coming on winter. She'll be at the height of her power, if you even reach her, traveling in the snow. Come inside. You can go in spring..."

Gerta stared at her. Did she really think that Gerta would go back in the house?

Does she think I'm stupid enough to trust her again?

"Are you mad?" she asked. "Do you think after all this—Are you *mad?*"

"I was keeping you safe!"

"I don't need to be safe!" Gerta could feel herself getting mad, but surely it was all right to be mad now, surely this, of all things, one could be mad about. "You kept me here for seven months! Kay could be *dead!*"

"He isn't dead," said Helga, her shoulders sagging. "The plants haven't seen him."

There were few plants left awake in the garden, but the long bare braids of the grapevines creaked when she spoke, a long, wordless sound, almost like assent.

"Good," said Gerta. Her voice sounded thick and strangled in her ears. "Good. I haven't failed yet."

She turned and began to walk toward the garden gate.

"Wait!" called Helga. "*Wait!*"

"Don't try to stop me," said Gerta. "Don't." She did not know what she would do if Helga did try—attack her, perhaps? She had never attacked anyone. Perhaps she would figure it out. If you hit a witch with your fists, did anything happen? Did magic stop you?

"I won't," said Helga. "I swear it. But it's starting to snow. It's nearly winter. You're not dressed for travel. If you wait just five minutes, I swear, not any longer, I'll get you a cloak."

"How do I know it won't be magicked?" said Gerta suspiciously. "I don't want to put it on and be under your spell again."

"It doesn't work like that," said Helga wearily. "I couldn't do that if I wanted to. I would if I could, to keep you here."

"How can I trust you, then?" asked Gerta.

Helga rubbed her hand over her face. "I will swear by anything you like," she said. "I will swear by the Blessed Virgin and the hosts of angels, by the soul of my mother, by the sacred pool where the witch-water is drawn. Give me five minutes, and let me give you a cloak to keep from freezing."

Gerta exhaled through her nose. She was cold, now that she was not working, cold, and her clothes did not fit as they had seven months ago. Her shirt gapped open between the buttons and had nearly worn through at the elbows.

In the seven months that she could barely remember, she had grown. And she had spent the nights dreaming of plants. Plants who had tried to help her.

Plants who might help her now.

She turned her head, not taking her eyes off Helga. "Reeds," she said. "Grapevine. Rowan tree. Is she telling the truth?"

She was aware on some level that she was asking plants for help, and how ridiculous that was. But she remembered the dreams and the green smell of chickweed and the rustle of rowan leaves overhead.

The grapevine creaked another long sound of assent. The reeds bent down as if they were nodding.

44

The rowan tree dropped a red berry at her feet. It was the color of the cords that her grandmother wrapped around Gerta's wrist when she was small, to protect against the folk of the woods.

Gerta exhaled.

"I won't put it on until I'm out of the garden," she told Helga. "And I'm staying right here by the gate. And I don't want you to touch me. But...all right."

"Very wise," said Helga bitterly, and went inside.

There must have been some magic involved. When she returned, she carried a luxurious fur muff and a heavy wool cloak. She had Helga's old pack slung over her shoulder.

"There's food in there," she said. "It's little enough, but it's not enchanted."

She set them down in the middle of the garden and retreated to the porch. Gerta took a deep breath, snatched them up, and hurried back to the gate.

Nothing terrible happened, and she did not feel any compulsion to return to the house.

"The Snow Queen will kill you," said Helga. "She'll reach into your heart and you'll feel like the lowest thing in the world. You'll kill yourself just to get away from being yourself."

"She has Kay," said Gerta grimly. She shouldered the pack. "I have to get him back."

Helga shook her head. "She'll kill you. Go home, if you can't stay here. The Snow Queen is a power beyond you."

Gerta closed the gate behind her.

When she was a good distance away, she stopped and clasped the cloak around her throat. It settled in heavy folds over her shoulders.

Nothing else happened.

She shoved her hands into the fur muff. It was very warm and a little of the desperation that had crawled into her heart at the thought of seven months passing eased.

She began walking north. Her last view of the farmhouse was of Helga standing among the empty vegetable beds with her hands over her face.

Chapter Eight

She slept that night in a haystack, because she was afraid to go up to a farmhouse. It was probably unlikely that they would also be witches, but she had lost far too much time.

Besides, how would I explain what I've been doing, or where I came from, or why my clothes don't fit?

The idea of trying to explain it all was too exhausting, and much too humiliating. She flushed with shame at the mere thought.

Hello, yes, I'm trying to find my true love, but I got enchanted for seven months but I'm better now. Can I buy some sausages?

Did she even deserve to call Kay her true love? She'd kissed him once, and certainly she loved him, but he deserved someone better. Someone who wouldn't get stuck at the very first house and lose seven months to a garden and a witch.

There was bread and cheese and ham in the pack, and a small bottle of water. She poured the water out and rinsed it in the stream before refilling it, just in case.

The food...well.

She was nearly faint with hunger by the time she stopped at the haystack. She sat down out of the wind, and opened her pack.

If I don't eat, I'll faint and fall down and freeze to death.

If I do eat, I may turn around and run back to Helga.

A few more snowflakes fell. The sky had not committed to snowing, but it was the color of iron and the wind was bitter cold.

One bite. I'll take one bite and see what happens.

She selected the ham, because it did not seem worth it to risk life and liberty for a bite of bread.

Well, it looks like ham…smells like ham…

It did not look or smell significantly magical. Perhaps it was difficult to enchant a ham.

She took the first bite, watching herself closely.

She did not turn around and run back to the garden. She stayed sitting with her back to the haystack.

A few minutes slid by, a few more snowflakes glided past, and she took another bite.

I suppose it might take effect once I sleep.

There was nothing much that she could do about that. She ate a frugal amount of bread and cheese and another bite of ham, then packed everything away and turned her attention to the haystack.

It was not as easy to dig into the stack as she had expected. The hay made her hands itch terribly and shed quantities of fine dust everywhere.

In the end, she did not so much hollow out a sleeping area as make a depression in the side, and cover the cold ground with hay. She curled into a tight ball with the cloak wrapped around her and the hood pulled down, partly to keep out the cold and partly to shield her from the godawful hay dust.

I know I've heard stories where people sleep in haystacks. I'm sure Grandmother told stories about that. Why didn't they ever mention how dusty it was?

Her dreams were the dreams of hay, of small animals rustling and the wind bending and the sun beaming. The hay had been cut, but it remembered being alive, and its dreams were all of summer.

Gerta woke in the morning, better rested than she probably deserved to be. Her back was sore, but she had not frozen to death. Given how the ground crackled with frost when she walked on it, this seemed like a victory.

She walked to the road. There was nothing in either direction but grey clouds and fields and frost. The hay's dreams were a small, warm ember in the back of her mind.

She walked on.

On the third day, she knew that she would have to stop. Her cloak was warm, if dusty, and the muff was marvelous for keeping her hands from freezing, but she was running low on food.

Chores, she thought. *I will offer to do chores. And I will not sleep in the house or drink anything they offer me, except for water.*

She gritted her teeth.

They can't possibly be witches, too. Every farmhouse between here and the North Pole is not inhabited by a witch. I was just very stupid and very unlucky.

The familiar flush of shame started up the back of her neck, and she waited it out grimly.

The farmhouse she chose was smaller than Helga's, and there were cobwebs on the porch. When she climbed up the steps, the boards creaked under her feet.

She stared at her hand and the door and lifted one to knock on the other, then lowered it again.

I have to knock. I'm being stupid. They can't all be witches.

But she did not have to knock. The door opened to reveal a girl only a few years older than herself, severely pregnant.

"I heard the steps," said the girl. "Can I help you?"

Gerta took a deep breath. "I'm traveling," she said. "I was hoping that I might do a few chores in return for a meal."

The girl's eyes moved over Gerta—the too-small clothing, the too-good muff and cloak, but she did not say anything. "I think we can manage that," she said. "The rugs need beating. It's heavy work and easier with two."

"Thank you," said Gerta.

They beat the rugs and then Gerta set to work with a broom, taking down the cobwebs on the porch. The windows were very small and the sills were very thick, and had acquired a coating of dead insects trying to get inside, away from the frost. She swept them away, the little brown husks pattering to the ground.

A few days ago—*and seven months*, she added mentally—she would have been squeamish about such work. Now it was simply an obstacle in her way to finding Kay, and she no longer had the luxury to worry about such obstacles.

"Thank you," said the girl, when Gerta returned. "You've been a help. I can't get around quite so easily at the moment."

Gerta smiled.

The girl fed Gerta a large lunch, with farmhouse cheese and bread stuffed with fish and a few apples. Gerta braced herself to decline tea or small beer, but she was apparently not considered an important enough guest for anything but water.

The girl wrapped another few apples up in a cloth, with a roll and a wedge of cheese. "It's a long way to the next town," she said, handing them over. Her eyes lingered again on the gaps in Gerta's clothing. "Did you leave someone's service?"

"Sort of," said Gerta. "It's…complicated."

"I will trade you a shirt," said the girl. She stood with her hand braced against her back, leaning back against the weight of her belly. "Mine's not such a good fabric as yours, but it will fit you better."

Gerta looked up, startled.

"People will think you've stolen that cloak," she said. "And perhaps you have, but it's no business of mine. I'd guess by the look of you that somebody turned you off without your wages. You worked hard for me, so whatever it was for, it wasn't shirking."

"I didn't steal it," said Gerta, licking dry lips.

"Then you'll do better with a shirt that fits," said the pregnant girl. "Otherwise people will wonder where you got the money for a cloak like that, when you can't afford a shirt."

Gerta bowed her head. "Thank you," she mumbled, feeling hot with embarrassment. How must she look, covered in hay dust, with her shirt hanging open?

She was glad to leave the house. Even though the girl had been kind enough, and more than fair in her payment for the work, it had been awkward.

The new shirt was rough homespun, and it did fit better, particularly across the chest. The girl had gotten a bargain, since Gerta's old shirt was linen, but there was no point in carrying around a linen shirt that didn't fit, particularly when it made her look like a servant girl who had been turned off from her employer without her wages.

She walked on.

Chapter Nine

It was a warm autumn day, the sort that can happen right into October. Gerta pushed her cloak back and put the muff in her pack.

The road surface was drier here, and walking was easier. Since she did not need to watch her feet, she looked around.

There was not a great deal of scenery. Trees marked the divisions between fields, and there was a blue band on the horizon that might be more trees. The fields were mown stubble and the weathered fences looked the same as weathered fences have looked since time immemorial. The ditches were full of dried grasses, which rattled in the breeze.

A few fields had a single tall tree in the middle, but not many. Her grandmother had said that such trees were sacred to Ukko, but perhaps no one cared about that any longer.

She kept an eye out for movement. Occasionally, a horse and rider would cross one of the fields, far away.

Mostly, though, she tried to remember the last seven months.

There was almost nothing left to her of those days, except for the dreams. She worried at it like a loose tooth, prodding from all angles, and was rewarded with fragments—a cup of tea, a fire, the red quilt covered in roses. Tying up beans and cutting down the withered stems of the peas.

There were slugs on the roses, she thought, staring over the landscape of brown and grey and white. *I picked slugs off the roses. But surely I didn't do that for an entire seven months!*

Even now, it was hard to believe that it had been so long. She did not even have a sense that time had passed.

But it was autumn. And her clothes no longer fit. Her breasts had grown, which was not entirely a blessing, and her thighs had thickened and her arms were more muscular. Her face, when she had seen it in the farm-wife's glass, was sharper around the cheekbones.

To her deep digust, she had not grown even a fraction of an inch taller.

Seven months. And all I have to show is dreams about plants. A whole spring and summer gone.

You only got so many springs and summers. Gerta stalked down the road, imagining herself as an old woman, looking back on those lost seasons, feeling robbed.

After awhile, she sighed and rubbed her forehead.

Well, so she had lost two seasons. So had Kay, presumably, since he was in the Snow Queen's clutches, and Gerta could not imagine that the Snow Queen lived anywhere but winter.

Being angry isn't getting me any closer to Kay. I just have to keep going. Maybe I'll remember more and it'll all come back to me.

She tried not to think about things that might have happened during her time in the witch's house, things that she might not *want* to remember.

She went on for most of a week, walking all day, hoping to reach the next town. The blue band proved to be a belt of trees, barely a hundred paces through. After that, there was nothing but fields.

She stopped at three more farmhouses.

Two of them were easy. The farmwife had children at both of them, and she was hailed with relief as another adult to talk to. (*Adult?* thought Gerta. *Me?*) She ate well and the second one even offered her a bath in a bucket of heated water, which Gerta accepted with gratitude.

The third house had a man living alone. He told her three times over supper that his wife had died and how lonely it was for him, and tried twice to touch her hair. His lower lip trembled when he talked. Gerta offered to sweep the porch, left a copper on the step to pay for her supper, and slipped away.

I may have spent the last seven months under a spell, she thought grimly, *but I'm not a total fool.*

The sun sank on her left. Gerta left the road, for the dubious comforts of another haystack.

She was tugging bits of hay into a nest when there was a flapping, fluttering noise, and a raven landed on the ground beside her.

Gerta raised her eyebrows. It was definitely not a crow. It was enormous and grey black. It tilted its head and looked at her with one bright eye, fluffing out a beard of narrow grey feathers.

"Are you hoping to share my dinner?" she asked. "Or pluck out my eyes?"

The raven hopped backward. "Auurk," it said. It had a deep rattlebone voice. "Auurk."

She tossed it a bit of bread.

It hopped closer, inspecting the bread. There was something wrong with one of its wings, she thought. It held the wing away from its body, not as if it were in pain, but as if it didn't bend quite properly.

It picked the bread up and swallowed it neatly. "Auurk."

"You're welcome." Gerta tossed it another crumb. It was strangely pleasant to have company that was not a human who might ask inconvenient questions. "What's wrong with your wing, bird?"

The raven looked up. "I broke it," it said simply.

Gerta's jaw dropped.

"You talk…" she said.

"So do you," said the raven. "Kudos all around. We are talking beings. Auurk."

"Is this magic?" asked Gerta, getting to her feet. "Are you another witch?" She would walk all night if she had to. Frostbite was nothing compared to being trapped by another magician.

"Aurk!" said the raven contemptuously. "Aurk! Ravens have spoken since Odin brought us to sit on his shoulders. My great-grandmother rode on the Morrigan's battle-harness. It is not our fault that humans are usually too cloddish to understand."

Gerta pulled her cloak tightly around her shoulders, not sure what to do next. "Then why can I understand you?"

The raven made a very derisive squawking noise. "*I'm* not doing anything," it said. "If you can hear me talk, it's all on you."

"Are you saying *I'm* doing something magical?" asked Gerta, baffled.

The raven turned its head to one side, then the other, fixing her with each eye in turn. "No," it said finally. "You haven't a drop in you. There's magic coating you like frost on a tree branch, that's all."

"But how do I get rid of it?" asked Gerta.

The raven spread its wings. The right one did not extend all the way, and moved stiffly when it flapped. "Shouldn't think you'd want to," it said. "Being able to talk to ravens is a sensible magic. Moreso than most of the fool stuff you see flying about. Aurrk!"

It leapt. Two ragged wingbeats and it was aloft, the stiff wing dipping. It flew low over the ground, to a fencepost, and landed.

"Wait—!" called Gerta, but the bird took off again and was gone.

Chapter Ten

Gerta saw the raven again the next day, when she stopped to eat. A small copse of birch trees kept the wind from cutting through, and when the road passed through, she decided to stop for a few minutes. She had been smelling snow in the air, but was hoping that she was wrong.

She sat with her back to the largest birch, alternating mouthfuls of bread and cheese.

The raven landed in front of her, light on its feet despite the awkward wing. "Aurk!"

Gerta eyed it suspiciously. It tilted its head and eyed her right back.

"Do you still talk?" she asked.

"Hell of a thing to forget in a day," said the raven. "Do you have any cheese?"

Gerta tossed a chunk of cheese to the bird. It snapped it up in a single bite and looked expectantly for more.

"Do you have a name?" asked Gerta.

"I do," said the raven.

Gerta waited.

The raven fluffed its beard. "I am the Sound of Mouse Bones Crunching Under the Hooves of God."

Gerta blinked a few times. "That's...quite a name."

"I made it myself," said the raven, preening. "I stole the very shiniest words and hoarded them all up until they made something

56

worth having. *Sound* and *God* were particularly well-guarded. *Crunching* I found in a squirrel nest, though."

"May I call you Mousebones?" asked Gerta. "It's...a lot to say all at once."

It was hard for a creature with a beak to scowl, but the raven managed, mostly with the skin around its eyes. "I suppose," it said. "If you *must.*"

"Mine's Gerta," said Gerta.

"There's your problem right there," said Mousebones. "Much too short and not enough in it. I don't know how you expect to become anything more than you are with a name like that."

Gerta put the bread and cheese away. The smell of snow was stronger, and she needed to move quickly if she wanted to find shelter by nightfall.

"Hugin and Munin," she said, looking straight ahead at the road, "the ravens who sit on Odin's shoulders, have names five letters long. Same as Gerta. They manage."

"Aurk! Aurk! Aurk!" laughed the raven. "Oh, aurk! Not bad for a fledgling human, not bad. Who told you that?"

"My grandmother," said Gerta. "She told me lots of stories. Fairy tales, mostly, but some about the old gods, too."

Her grandmother had been a good Christian, as everyone in Gerta's village was, but she loved a story and so Gerta had grown up on tales of Thor and Loki and Sampson and Martin Luther all tangled together like rumpled knitting.

"Aurk." Mousebones hopped from fencepost to fencepost beside her, keeping pace. "You have no magic in you, you know, not even the little bits that come down because somebody's great-great-grandsire crossed a fairy mound the wrong direction."

Gerta tried not to feel insulted.

"You get it from your grandmother, I imagine," said Mousebones. "That's a guess. Only a guess, but a raven's guess is worth more than a magpie's. Aurrk!"

"Get what?" asked Gerta.

"No magic," said Mousebones. "When it's that strong, being unmagical is a thing itself. Like being a white raven. White ravens aren't really white, they're just an absence of black. But they're very good at it."

This did not make a great deal of sense to Gerta, but asking questions would probably just make things even more muddled.

There was also the small fact that she was talking to a raven, which was clearly a strange thing to do. Ravens were very canny birds, everyone knew, but they didn't talk. Not to mortals, anyway.

And I am not a fairy and most definitely not a god. Gerta tried to think if any other class of people talked to ravens. *Witches, maybe. Saints.*

She did not think that she was a witch. She would have rather liked to be a saint, but saints tended to come to a bad end. *Perhaps I'll be martyred by the Snow Queen…*

If the coming snow caught her outside of shelter, she would be martyred by the weather, and the Snow Queen wouldn't have to bother.

It was probably not worth wondering if she was mad. She was already chasing after Kay, who had been abducted by a woman in a sleigh pulled by white otters. If she had gone mad, it had obviously been months ago, and there was no point in worrying about it now.

She kept walking.

Mousebones flew down the road a little way ahead of her, to root around in the ditch. When she drew abreast, the raven made a great hop and landed on her pack. Gerta grunted, more from surprise than the weight. It was the size of a cat, but very light.

"Mousebones?"

"Aurk?"

"Are you a he-raven or a she-raven?"

"I am a raven," said Mousebones, "and the rest is none of your business, as we'll not be having eggs together."

"Sorry," said Gerta. "I just…it's awkward thinking of you as 'it.'"

"Oh no, a human feeling awkward. How *terrible.*"

Gerta flushed scarlet. *Do saints blush? What about witches?*

Mousebones tilted its head, opened its beak and carefully gripped her ear.

"What are you doing? Stop that!" Gerta ducked her head. It had felt like blunt scissors on her skin.

"It turned so red, I couldn't resist," said the raven. "Was that a blush? White ravens don't do that."

Gerta mumbled something. She had thought that it would be less embarrassing to talk to a bird than a human, but apparently not.

She put her head down and walked very fast.

After a dozen fenceposts had gone by, Mousebones said "Sorry. You're only a fledgling and out of the nest a bit too soon, aren't you?"

Gerta shrugged. The raven sank its talons into her pack and flapped to keep balance.

"The other human girl I know isn't much older than you, but she came out of the egg with all her pinfeathers. I'm being rude." Mousebones picked up a lock of hair in its beak and preened it down, which felt even stranger than its beak on her ear had.

"Thanks," said Gerta, almost inaudibly. She wondered who the other girl Mousebones knew was—had she handled a talking raven better?

"You may call me he," said Mousebones, "for 'it' is an ugly word. I may feel differently later, but I will inform you first." He groomed another bit of her hair. "Are we well, Gerta?"

It had an air of ritual to it, even with the informality of the words.

"We're well, Mousebones," she answered.

"Good."

Chapter Eleven

The snow that night came quietly at first, a few flakes and a few more flakes, then settled into a business-like snow that did not trouble itself with theatrics. The winds did not howl and the flakes did not dance. They simply fell straight down, thick and white and relentless.

There were no haystacks. There were no farmhouses. Gerta had been watching for one for hours, and there were none. The fields were grey and barren. The last house had been four hours ago, before she stopped for lunch.

Even the fences had ended. Gerta had a grim feeling that she had walked out of the fields and into moorland.

"Should I have gone back?" she asked Mousebones.

"Does it matter?" asked the raven. "You didn't go back." He shook himself, and snowflakes fell off his shining black feathers. "Snow. I never liked snow."

"I thought birds spent the winter in the land of the dead," said Gerta.

"Aurk!" He gave her a suspicious look. "Who told you that?"

She shrugged. "I don't know. Everyone, I guess."

"Nobody I know," said the raven. "*I've* certainly never been to the land of the dead." He considered this. "Maybe sparrows. Sparrows always seem like they know more than they're telling." He flew to a fencepost and fluffed his beard briefly.

Gerta shoved her hands deeper into the fur muff. At first she left small, melted boot-prints on the road.

After a time, they no longer melted and she left white prints on white. The wind began to pick up but the snow fell as thick as ever.

If the snow had been deeper, she would have been in better spirits. Every child in the village knew how to build a snow cave and hunker down in it—it was one of the things you learned about winter, like throwing yourself flat on ice that started to crack, like watching out for icicles that might fall off the eaves and drive themselves into your skull.

But a few inches of cold, wet snow were different than two feet of dry, packable snow. Gerta took a deep breath and felt the cold like knives in her chest.

"It is possible that I am going to die," she said. She wanted to feel badly about this, but her nose was running in the cold and it was hard to concentrate on her own death when she felt as if she might drown in snot. She wiped furiously at her nose and wished for a handkerchief.

"It is a certainty that you are going to die," said Mousebones. "All living things die. Then we eat their eyes."

"How nice," said Gerta. "Are you going to eat my eyes?"

"Well, obviously. You'd want a friend to do it, wouldn't you?" Mousebones groomed a snowflake off her hair. "And it's not like you'd be *using* them."

Gerta sighed and wiped her nose on her sleeve again. The inside of her nostrils felt raw.

"However," said Mousebones, "since you have given me cheese and carried me all this way, I will not eat your eyes today, unless you want me to."

"*Want* you to?"

"Well," said Mousebones, fluffing up all his feathers and settling them again. "Some people do. For wisdom, you know. I could pluck out an eye and eat it and then the other one would have the second sight. In theory."

"Does that work?" asked Gerta.

Mousebones made a drawn out *aaaurrrrr-rrr-rrk* sound. "It might," he said, a bit doubtfully. "I just handle the eye-eating bit. The second sight is somebody else's problem."

Gerta could think of nothing to say to that.

"I don't know why people want second sight anyway," the raven added. "You'd think seeing *one* world would be enough."

"I might give an eyeball if I could see a haystack right now," said Gerta, sighing. It seemed unlikely. Visibility had plunged and now the world was grey and white only a few yards off the road. Even if there were mysterious mobile haystacks lurking in the moors, she wouldn't be able to see them.

The raven launched himself into the air. Gerta ducked her head, startled. "That wasn't an offer!" she yelled after him.

Mousebones paid her no heed. She could see the stiffness in his bad wing as he flapped away into the snow.

She tried not to feel bereft. Presumably a raven could roost in a tree somewhere and not freeze to death. She couldn't. There was no reason Mousebones should stay with her and freeze.

Gerta had pulled the hood of her cloak low and her face was wet where her breath steamed up into it. She definitely was not crying. It would be stupid to cry about a raven.

"He'd only have eaten my eyes anyway," she said glumly.

The snow grew thicker and thicker. It was no longer crunching underfoot, but piling up silently. Gerta felt as if the world was growing larger and larger, or as if she were growing smaller and more insignificant, a little hooded mouse toiling along the road, not even leaving tracks behind her.

She stopped and pushed her hood back. The wind cut at her wet cheeks and froze her eyelashes.

She could see the road ahead and behind, and nothing else.

I am going to freeze. I could walk ten feet from a farmhouse and never know.

She could taste despair on her tongue, like dust.

I might as well lie down in the snow and get it over with. At least it will be painless. They say freezing is the best way to die.

And then, from overhead, she heard the high, familiar chime of bells.

Chapter Twelve

Gerta looked up.

All she could see at first was white snow rushing at her from a pale grey sky. It was a dizzying perspective, and for a moment she felt queasy, as if the snow was still and the ground was rocketing upward.

Then a shape passed overhead, white-on-grey, eerily silent except for the chiming bells. The white otters poured through the sky, running on air as easily as they had run on snow. The sled cut a long path through the sky, leaving a snowless wake behind it.

Gerta was below and a little to the left. She could not see much of the interior from her angle, but the Snow Queen stood in the front of the sled, and behind her, dark-haired and wrapped in furs, but with his head bare—

"Kay!" cried Gerta. *"Kay!"*

He did not look at her. Perhaps he did not hear.

The Snow Queen heard, though, and as the sled ran past, she turned her head.

Her single glance fell over Gerta like a blow.

—*mewling, red-faced, mortal, stinking of sweat*—

Gerta staggered and went to one knee under the weight of her own uselessness.

The Snow Queen's gaze flicked away. Gerta gasped for air, feeling the cold stab her lungs, and what did it matter, none of it mattered, she should lie down and die the snow was clean and she was filthy but if it covered her over no one would see what a wretched creature she was and that was the best that she could ever hope for.

"No," said Gerta. She had to bite the word and spit it out. "*No. I can't die now. Someone needs to help Kay.*"

Kay is alive. I just saw him. If I am a wretched, filthy creature, so be it. I don't have be anything else. I just have to get to Kay.

Kay deserves better than me, but I'm all there is.

The thought got her back to her feet. Her knee was soaked through from kneeling in the snow and the backs of her hands were burning.

She found the fur muff and shoved her hands in it. Walking... yes. That was next. She could walk.

She stumbled forward.

Mousebones found her a few minutes later and landed on her pack. "Well," he said. "*That* was something. Did you see the crazy sled pulled by otters?"

"The Snow Queen," croaked Gerta, too broken to realize that Mousebones had returned. "She has Kay. I have to get him back, but I'm going to freeze to death."

"You don't sound so good," said the raven.

Gerta took a deep breath and then a swallow of water from her flask. It was slushy with ice and chilled her deeply, but her lips and tongue moved more easily for it. "She looked at me," she said. "It's...I think it's something she does. Did she look at you?"

Mousebones raised his head. "I should say she did. I nearly flew into her."

Gerta turned her head. She could just see the long, wicked beak alongside her cheek. "And when she did, you didn't...you didn't feel..."

She paused, trying to find the words. "Dirty," she said finally, feeling even more wretched for not being able to describe it. "Mortal. Awful, compared to her."

"Aur-*k*," said Mousebones. "Compared to her, I'm a raven. And ravens do not bow to gods or men or giants." He lifted his head proudly, and Gerta felt even worse. She was not a raven. A little cat-sized bundle of feathers and bone could stand before the Snow Queen and she could not.

She trudged on in silence.

"Anyway," said Mousebones, after a minute, "there's a stand of bushes about a hundred feet farther up. It's the only cover we're going to get, and this storm goes on in both directions for a long time, so I suggest you stop there."

Gerta blinked.

It occurred to her, rather sluggishly, that she might not freeze to death. This was an interesting idea, although she did not have much energy left to be interested.

"You can cut some branches to perch on," said Mousebones. "And then we'll roost together, so we don't freeze to death, and I will be on my very best behavior and won't pluck out even *one* eye."

He sounded as if he were making a great sacrifice, and Gerta choked out a laugh. The cold inside her thawed a tiny bit.

The bushes were only a little way down the road, nearly covered in drifting snow. They were white lumps on white ground and she had to look carefully to see them.

"Odin's forehead," grumbled Mousebones. "Aurk! They were green when I saw them before. It's coming down hard."

The bushes were barely waist high, but it was enough. Gerta pulled her knife and hacked off a half-dozen branches from the bottom of the largest. They were some kind of low evergreen— junipers, she thought. The smell, even through the cold, was sharp and clean.

Mousebones flapped and bounced in the snow while she excavated a gap in the bushes. She laid the branches down on the ground to provide an inch of insulation between her and the snow, then crawled underneath the bush.

It was still cold, but being out of the wind made a startling difference. Snow still slid from the branches overhead every time

Gerta moved, but presumably it would settle down eventually. She pulled her hood low over her face and tucked her knees up.

Mousebones hopped inside and climbed up on her shoulder. "Not the best night roost," he grumbled. "I've seen better."

"Sorry," said Gerta. "It's what we've got."

"Aurk."

She was very tired. She ate a few bites of food and drank a few swallows of water. When the village children were taught what to do if you were trapped out in the snow, their teachers had always been very clear that you had to keep eating and drinking or you would die much faster.

Gerta sighed. She did not know if she had done it right. They talked about snow caves and this was a little like a cave but she had never actually built one for real. She didn't know if she'd wake up with dead toes or if she'd even wake up at all.

Junipers were supposed to be tough. Her grandmother said that the family was made of juniper, stubborn right down to the bone. She did not feel particularly tough or stubborn or anything else.

"Aurk!" said Mousebones. "Stop fidgeting."

"Sorry," said Gerta. She tucked her hands into her armpits. *Will they find my body in the spring thaw…?*

It was her last thought before she fell asleep.

Chapter Thirteen

She dreamed the dreams of evergreens with snow on them. The air smelled sharply of resin. A woman rode by her, on a grey horse that stumbled. She was talking to herself, or to the horse, but the language was strange.

Gerta would have liked to follow the woman, to see if she knew where to take shelter from the snow, but she and the horse vanished into the trees, hidden by the snow. Gerta sighed.

The snow began to melt around her. It ran in rivulets over last year's leaves. Pale green needles flushed out on the tips of the branches.

"Spring?" said Gerta. She turned.

A child was staring at her from beside a tree trunk, a child with pasty, swollen skin. It had blank black eyes, the pupils grotesquely dilated, a thin rim of iris around them. It stared at her with its mouth hanging open.

Gerta jerked back, revolted, and woke herself up.

"Aurk!" said Mousebones, flapping for purchase on her shoulder. One wing clipped her on the back of the head. "Aurk! What was that?"

"Nightmare," said Gerta. Was that her own dream, or the junipers? She couldn't tell the difference anymore.

"I should say so. You squawked like a jay with her egg being stolen."

Gerta scrubbed a hand over her face. It was still wet from her breath melting over it. "Sorry."

Mousebones made a sound that would have been a chirp in a smaller bird. "Rrrrk. I suppose I will not get to eat your eyes today, at least."

Before Gerta could comment (and what would she say?), Mousebones hopped off her shoulder. Branches had leaned down inside the bush, sagging with the weight of the snow. There was a raven-sized gap at the bottom and Mousebones ducked through it, leaving rune-shaped tracks behind him.

"Aurk!" Gerta heard. "Aurk! Come out, the snow's stopped."

Gerta slithered out from under the bush.

The snow had indeed stopped. Gerta turned, looked in every direction, and saw whiteness. Sun dazzled the edges of her vision. She had to squint, but she was glad of it, because without the sun, she would have had no idea which direction she had come from, and which way she should be going. Her footsteps had filled in overnight.

She could see the road, which was higher than the surrounding moor. The scruffy bushes she had slept in were one of a dozen small shapes dotting the landscape, all of them smoothed over by drifted snow.

"Mousebones?" she said.

The raven was rolling on his back in the snow, kicking his feet. He looked thoroughly undignified and thoroughly unconcerned about it. "Aurk?"

"Do you know how far it is to the next town?"

Mousebones stood up and sloughed snow off his feathers. "Not that far. I could fly it, even with my wing, and not be sore in the morning."

"All right," said Gerta.

She had a brief breakfast, which she shared with her bird companion. The ham was gone. The cheese was going. She still had money, which did her no good at all out on the moors.

If I can get to the town, I can buy supplies at least.

It took until noon before she saw a blue blot on the horizon. Walking in the sun was warm, but the wind was cold. Gerta flipped her hood up every few minutes and pulled the cloak forward over her arms, but then she would overheat and flip it back again.

"Make up your mind," grumbled Mousebones, who didn't like moving whenever she rearranged her cloak.

"Sorry," said Gerta. "It's too hot inside and too cold outside."

"Humans! Aurk! No pleasing you. Grow feathers, why don't you?"

Gerta snorted. "And then what? I'd be a big feathery thing. I still couldn't fly, could I?"

"No, but you'd be better looking."

"I'll pass, thanks."

The blue blot grew, separated into smaller, squarer blots, and became a town. Gerta walked into it in the middle of the afternoon.

The houses were small, with thick walls and sharply sloped roofs to slide the snow off. A few clustered tight together in the center of town, but more straggled off in all directions. Garden plots were covered in a blanket of snow.

It was a much smaller town than Gerta's home, but the little details—cut-outs on the shutters and the overhangs, elaborately carved benches—suggested prosperity.

Or at least very long winters. When you don't have much else to do, you might as well carve things…

The town was bustling despite the recent snowfall. Fresh sled tracks marked the street.

She had gone perhaps a dozen yards into the village proper when she realized that people were staring at her.

One man stood with his mouth hanging open, swiveling his head as she passed. Small children pointed and whispered to each other.

Gerta blushed hotly at first, checking her clothing—was her shirt gaping open? Was she so obviously out of place?

Then she remembered that she had a raven perched on her pack, and the heat faded from her cheeks. *Ah. Yes. That.*

If people wanted to stare because of Mousebones, she couldn't blame them. She wouldn't tell the raven to leave, though. If it hadn't been for him, Gerta would have stumbled past the bushes without seeing them.

Assuming I didn't just lie down in the snow to die when I saw the Snow Queen... Gerta lowered her chin and went looking for the local inn.

Chapter Fourteen

The inn was quiet. The evening rush had not yet descended. There was a great deal of warm, polished wood, and a mellow quiet.

An old woman was sitting next to the fire. She was really truly old, older than Gerta's grandmother. Her hair lay in thin, straggling wisps.

"Come in," she said, when Gerta paused on the doorstep. "You'll let the heat out."

And when Gerta had come inside, with Mousebones on her shoulder—"Look at you!"

"Everyone else is," said Gerta dryly.

The old woman cackled, a really *good* cackle, the sort that you can only get if you are over the age of eighty and know how to drink.

"Sit down," she said. "You could use a bite to eat, I bet, or your black-winged friend could."

"It's true," said Mousebones.

"Caw!" said the old woman, and cackled again.

Gerta had one very surreal moment when it seemed that Mousebones was speaking a human language and the old woman was speaking like a raven. Then the woman said, "Caw to you, too!" and Gerta realized that she was imitating Mousebones.

"Her accent is atrocious," said the raven haughtily.

"I'm sure he'd like something," said Gerta, sitting. "But I can pay…"

The old woman shook her head. "Nothing doing!" she said. "You've paid me already. They'll all come in tonight, you know, to ask me for your story."

Gerta rubbed her forehead. "I'm sorry, ma'am, I don't understand."

"I'm the storyteller," said the old woman. "Gran Aischa. My daughter runs this place." She banged her mug on the little table beside her. "Ebba! Ebba, come here, and bring this girl and her bird some sausages!"

A tall, stoop-shouldered woman came from the back, looked at Gerta, looked at Mousebones, rolled her eyes, and went into the back.

A few minutes later, she re-emerged with a plate of sausages. "I hope your bird is housetrained," she said.

"Nope!" said Mousebones happily.

Gerta winced and moved her chair so that Mousebones had his tail over the hearthstones instead of the wooden floor.

The sausages were small and spicy and delicious. Gerta handed every third one up to Mousebones, who took them from her fingertips as neatly as if he were plucking out someone's eyeballs.

Gran Aischa watched her while she ate, her bright eyes moving from her face to Mousebones on her shoulder. It would have been uncomfortable, but the old woman kept up a string of chatter about the town—commentary about the snow coming down so early in the year (but not so early as the one winter, when it snowed all through the harvest) and some foolish farmer who hadn't brought the cows in early and had to go out in the snow with a lantern to find them.

Gerta said nothing, and let the flow of words wash over her, until she was full of sausages and potatoes and cider.

"Good?" asked Gran Aischa. "All the corners filled in?"

"Very good," said Gerta.

"I forgive her the accent," said Mousebones, "if her daughter can cook such sausages."

The storyteller smiled, and her eyes nearly vanished in the swirl of wrinkles.

"Good!" she said. "Very good. Now…about your story…"

"Do you want to know *my* story?" asked Gerta, somewhat amused. "So you can tell it?"

"Not particularly," said the old woman. "No one wants true stories. They want stories with truth dusted over them, like sugar on a bun." She cackled again. "But tell me a little bit of yours anyway."

Gerta considered.

My friend was stolen away by the Snow Queen and I went after him and then I got caught by a witch and stayed for seven months and don't remember much of anything and now I can understand ravens— well, that was true, so far as it went, but it wouldn't actually sound all that sane coming out of her mouth.

Then again, here I am with a raven…

"My friend is missing," she said finally. "I think he was—ah—kidnapped. I've been searching for him, but I was—er—delayed. For a few months. But now I'm looking again."

"Your friend?" said Gran Aischa. "Or your true love?"

"Both," said Gerta firmly.

"Better!" Gran Aischa grinned, revealing a surprisingly good set of teeth for her age. "Ah, let me see, how should the story go… You're a princess, of course."

"I am?"

"Naturally." Gran Aischa swatted her on the knee. "You can hardly do anything worthwhile in a story unless you're a princess, you know."

"That doesn't seem very fair," said Gerta, taking a sip of the cider. Her mouth crooked up at the corners despite herself.

"It isn't," said the storyteller. "But you're young. Old women can be wise, but young women have to be princesses."

"I'm a bit short for a princess. And a bit…err…round…."

Gran Aischa waved away this objection. "Doesn't matter. Once you've left town, all they'll remember is what I tell them. You'll be devastatingly beautiful within a week. They were mostly looking at the raven, anyway."

Gerta laughed.

"Ye-e-e-s….yes, I see it now. You're a very clever princess. Your advisor, the raven, has told you all the wisdom in the world."

Mousebones preened. "I like this story."

"That's right, I'm talking about you, bird." Gran Aischa took a sip of her own drink. Gerta suspected it was rather stronger than cider. "You've learned wisdom from the raven, and nowhere is there a prince worthy of you. Men are tongue-tied in your presence. They present themselves to you in your palace and they can't remember a single word."

Gerta dragged her hand over her face. "All right," she said. "Where's this palace of mine, anyhow?"

"Oh, very far away. A year and a day by horse."

"How inconvenient for me."

"It's a magnificent palace," the storyteller assured her. "Each hall more extraordinary than the last. The walls are hung with rose-colored satin and the ceilings hung with chips of cut glass. You rule from a throne inlaid with diamonds and drink from a cup inlaid with pearls."

"Constantly," said Gerta.

"But alas, it is lonely when you are unmarried, and none of the princes who come before you can speak a single word."

Gerta put her chin on her hand and waited.

"You got tired of waiting around for a worthy husband to present himself," continued Gran Aischa, "so you went out, with your trusted raven, to find the prince wise enough to speak to you without fear." She brought her hands together. "And you are still looking, but one day, I'm sure, you'll find him."

"I hope so!" said Gerta, more fervently than she intended to.

"And he will be as handsome as the dawn and wear red and he will keep ravens of his own. And your beautiful bird will meet his mate as well, and the two of them will be kept as official court ravens and fed all the best bits from the kitchen."

("Get the sausage recipe from the innkeeper, will you?" asked Mousebones. "I want the palace kitchens to make these sausages.")

"And you and your wise prince will talk long into the night, every night, and live to a ripe old age. And the children in this town will grow up telling the story of how they saw the Raven Princess, before she found her prince."

Gerta grinned ruefully. "It's a better story than the truth," she admitted. "Though I still don't think anyone's going to believe I'm beautiful. Or wise."

"People will believe anything if you add enough details they like," said Gran Aischa. "It's a good story. Thank you for bringing it to me." She reached out with her mug and clinked it against Gerta's.

"Although," she added, taking a long slug of her drink, "I won't swear that I won't add to it, if it's early in the evening. A comic case of mistaken identity, say, or three tasks, or a riddle game." She glanced up at Mousebones. "Ravens and riddle games go well together, I always thought."

"It's true," said Mousebones, wiping his beak on Gerta's hair. "I know lots of riddles, and not just the stupid one about writing desks."

"So long as you don't give me a tragic ending," said Gerta. "Please?"

Gran Aischa laughed. "No, I like you. I won't have you starve to death in the snow while your prince marries another. I save that for rude people."

"Good to know."

Gerta finished her cider and stretched her hands to the fire. The silence was companionable and the room was warm. Perhaps that was why she felt comfortable asking the next question aloud.

"Gran Aischa—in all your stories, have you heard of the Snow Queen?"

Chapter Fifteen

The old woman looked up, startled. Her wispy hair shook around her face. "What?"

"The Snow Que—"

"Hsst! I heard you." She made silencing gestures with her hands, as gnarled and thin as Mousebones' talons. "Careful with that name. I don't know if she's one of the spirits that hears when you speak of them, but I don't know that she's not."

"She already knows I exist," said Gerta. "But I won't talk about her if you'd rather not."

Gran Aischa picked her mug up, then set it down again untasted. "That's a darker story than I made for you," she said. "Much darker. It's not one I'd tell often, and not in winter."

Gerta bowed her head.

"How did you run afoul of that fell maid?"

"She took my friend," said Gerta. "Stole him in the night. I saw them go, but I didn't follow soon enough…"

Gran Aischa frowned. She got up then and went to the bar and poured herself out another drink. The smell of it, when she came back to the fire, was thin and raw and potent.

"Let him go," she said.

"I'm sorry?"

"Your friend," said Gran Aischa. "That's a story with no happy ending. You've still got a chance at yours." She drank deeply and grimaced. "Let him go. Find yourself a strapping lad who knows how to listen and will worship the ground you walk on. They're rare, but they're worth it."

"But she kidnapped him!" said Gerta. "I can't just abandon him!" She flushed with shame at the thought that she had done so for seven months already.

Gran Aischa shook her head. "She doesn't take the unwilling. He had to climb into her sledge himself."

"I'm sure she enchanted him somehow—he wouldn't have—"

She had to stop then, remembering how Kay had always loved the snow and the cleanness of it, and how beautiful the Snow Queen looked. Yes. Perhaps he had climbed into the sledge himself.

"She'll kill him," she said.

Gran Aischa sighed. "Oh, eventually. She'll give him kisses—and more than kisses—and all that ice will work its way to his heart. But he'll never feel a thing."

"I can't let that happen!"

"Plenty of sweethearts die as children," said the storyteller. "They fall through the ice or cross a pasture with a bull or catch a fever and die of it. It's hard and there's tears, but you shouldn't throw your life away pining for them." She smoothed her hair down. "Your sweetheart's gone, same as if he'd died of a fever. Running after him won't help."

"Please," said Gerta. "If you know anything…if there's anything you can tell me…"

She dropped to her knees in front of the fire.

Gran Aischa sighed and looked down at Gerta. "You're asking me to hand you the knife," she said bitterly, "so you can go fall on it. I shouldn't tell you anything. But you ask very prettily and I'm too old to stop foolish children any longer."

She gestured impatiently to Gerta, who climbed back into her chair and perched on the edge, leaning far forward.

"That one," said Gran Aischa. "*That one* lives farther north than north, and you won't get there on a human road. You'll need to find another way." Her eyes rested on Mousebones for a moment.

"Still, walking north with a raven on your shoulder is a good start. Keep your eyes closed and your heart open. The way will open, or it won't. You'll know if it doesn't, if you come at last to the sea."

She took another sip. "*That one* delights in the cold and oversees it. I knew an old Sámi woman—long and long ago it was. She might be dead now. She told me *that one* was not one of their spirits, but they knew of her, for all that they're good Christians now."

Gran Aischa frowned into her drink. "I've heard a great many stories about her, but you know that stories are not always true. Some say she was a human girl unlucky in love and it froze her heart, and now she searches the world for pretty boys to freeze in turn." She shook her head. "I doubt that. The shape of her in my head is not human, and I've learned to trust such things. I think she was a spirit born of ice and she steals away human children. Cut from the same cloth as the Fair Folk, anyway."

Gerta shook her head, puzzled.

"Creatures of the south," said Gran Aischa. "They live a little outside the world and steal people from our world into theirs. When the plagues came so long ago, most of the people died, but I imagine the Fair Folk lived." She took another drink. "I won't get to the great port again in my lifetime, or I'd ask a trader there if they still put out milk for the fairies. I'd be surprised if they didn't." She leaned forward and poked a withered finger at Gerta. "Not like us. The tonttu were never as cruel as the Fair Folk."

Gerta nodded politely. The old storyteller was rambling now, and Gerta wasn't sure if there was much more sense to be gotten from her. Her grandmother had put out hot oatmeal for the tonttu, the spirits of the house and the sauna, but those little household magics were a long way from the Snow Queen.

"Stay the night," said Gran Aischa abruptly, her eyes sharpening. "Stay and sleep well, and have a good meal. Go in the sauna and bake the sorrow out of your bones. It may be the last chance you get. And in the morning, when you walk north with your raven—well. If you walk all the way to Sápmi on this road, look for a woman named Livli. She used to live just over the border. She was old then and will be older now, but some women age like tree roots and last nearly forever."

Gerta's heart sank at the thought of walking clear to Sápmi—how far would that even be?

Still, for Kay. If I must walk to the end of the world, so be it. Sápmi is not so far, compared to that. And I will have a meal and not have to sleep under a hedge tonight.

"I would be glad to stay," she said.

"If you do meet Livli," said Gran Aischa, "tell her that your story is written on the hides of herring. She'll find that funny." She smiled herself, but it was sad, and did not quite touch her eyes.

Her dreams that night were quiet. She stayed in the sauna until she could not stop from yawning, and slept immediately.

The wooden floor and the long wooden ceiling beams had been an inn far longer than they had been trees. Their dreams were of polishing and dust motes and footsteps, and overwhelmingly of travelers sleeping. So Gerta slept and in her dreams she slept again, and she woke feeling strong and hungry.

Gran Aischa's daughter fed her an enormous meal of spiced sausages and eggs and onions, and sent her on her way with a pack that groaned with food.

"What do I owe you?" asked Gerta, reaching for the small pouch of coins at her side.

"You don't," said the storyteller's daughter. "My mother tells me that you are going to your death, and we don't charge the dying for their last meals."

Gerta blinked. On her shoulder, Mousebones shifted from foot to foot.

"Mother is not very tactful," said the innkeeper, sighing. "But she sees a long way, when she can see at all. Be careful. You could stay here, you know. I can always use a hand around the inn."

Gerta shook her head. "It's very kind of you," she said, "and I appreciate it. But I have to find Kay."

"Then go with God," said the storyteller's daughter, "and whatever kindly spirits you meet along your path."

Chapter Sixteen

She and Mousebones had been on the road for two days when the raven said "The other human girl I knew lives near here."

Gerta felt a pang of something that wasn't jealousy, but was at least a little like it. "Oh?" she said, keeping her voice carefully neutral.

"In the woods," said Mousebones, gesturing toward the line of trees off to their left. "She lives there with her flock."

Gerta's first instinct, rapidly squelched, was to walk away from the forest.

That's stupid. We're friends, that's all, and he's allowed to have other friends.

She aimed her feet toward the trees. "Do you think she'll let us stay for the night?"

"I stayed for weeks," said Mousebones. "She healed up my wing and fed me dead mice."

"...hopefully she'll have something for humans to eat, too."

It occurred to Gerta that Mousebones might prefer to spend the winter in the care of a healer who fed him dead mice. She felt an odd wash of cold from the center of her chest at the thought.

He's not my pet. If he wants to stay there, he can.

And if the thought of not having him around to hunger after my eyeballs makes me feel a bit like crying...well, that's my problem, not his.

Aloud, she said only "It'll be warmer there than it will be in a ditch, I'm sure."

It took an hour to reach the trees, but she was glad that she had started in that direction. The sky was developing a certain grey heaviness that she didn't like. It looked like more snow was on the way.

There was a clear gap in the trees. She made for it and found the remnants of a road.

Mousebones took off, winging awkwardly from tree to tree. Gerta bit her lip.

Don't be stupid. He wouldn't leave without saying goodbye.

And indeed, a few minutes later he returned, shaking snow down on her and cawing laughter.

"Hey! That's cold!"

"Aurk!"

She tossed a snowball at him underhand, and he flew easily out of the way, snickering.

"You're lucky you've got wings," she said.

"Wings are the natural state of being," he said. "You were just born unlucky." He hopped onto a bough overhead. "The other human lives near here. Follow me."

Gerta followed him. Pine needles crunched underfoot as she walked.

Don't be so nervous. This is no different than a farmhouse, and you got used to going up to those. If you don't like her, you can leave.

But would Mousebones come with me?

"Not far now—" called Mousebones, and then a large man stepped out from behind a tree and grabbed Gerta around the waist.

Gerta yelped. "Hey—*hey!*"

He was very large and red-faced, with stubble more yellow than grey. He looked at her for a moment with his brow knit, and then he bent his knees and heaved her into the air.

"*Stop—!*" Gerta began, and then he had her slung over his shoulder and was jogging through the forest.

84

She had never been slung over anyone's shoulder before. It had very little to recommend it. Her head was hanging down and the ground was lurching past.

"Aurk!" she heard Mousebones calling. "Aurk! Stop that! Put my human down! You don't carry other humans that way!"

She tried kicking her feet but could get no leverage. She elbowed him in the kidneys and he grunted, so she did it again, but he didn't slow down.

The other problem with being carried like that became rapidly apparent. Every step slammed his shoulder into her gut, over and over. Things started to move, and not in a good way.

Gerta tried to get a hand over her mouth, but it wasn't going to do any good, so then she just tried to get her hand out of the way.

She threw up.

He stopped.

She was furious and frightened and also embarrassed. It was stupid to be embarrassed about throwing up on someone when you had just been picked up and manhandled against your will, but she was anyway.

The red-faced man slung her off his shoulder and tossed her to the ground.

There was no snow to cushion her fall, only hard earth. She landed badly and the air went out of her.

What little she could see, in between wheezing, was a hard packed courtyard and a building like a pigeon coop. It looked shabby and half-falling down.

"Goddamn, Marten," someone said over her head. "What have you done?"

The red-faced man—Marten?—said, "She was in the woods." His voice was very deep.

"People are *allowed* to be in the woods."

"She was nosin' around. Looked to walk right in here."

"So you decided to make absolutely *sure* she found us. How useful."

The speaker walked into Gerta's line of sight.

She was tall and lean and not much older than Gerta herself. Her skin was dark brown and her hair was blacker than Mousebones' feathers. She wore a bright scarf around her shoulders.

Gerta recognized her immediately.

The girl reached down a hand and pulled Gerta to her feet.

"It's you," said Gerta stupidly, still clutching her hand. She was aware that she was streaked with vomit and her hair was hanging in rags and she felt embarrassed again, because she would have wanted to make a better impression.

The other girl turned her head slightly, suddenly wary. "Do we know each other?"

"From my dream," said Gerta. She could feel the blush coming on because what she was saying was dreadfully stupid, but the words kept coming out and there was no stopping them. "The grapevine dream. I saw you. You were in it, with the wood-pigeons."

This is not something normal people say to strangers. Now you'll have to explain about the witch and then explain that you were stupid enough to be enchanted for months and incidentally you've sort of been kidnapped, and probably you should worry about that instead—

Her face was burning, clear to the tips of her ears. She wiped her hand across her mouth, feeling unutterably foolish, and yet this was without a doubt the woman that she had seen in the dream given to her by the grapevines.

"Wood-pigeons," said the girl slowly. "Yes. I keep wood-pigeons."

"She's got money," said Marten. "Or a little jingly pouch, anyway. And her pack's full and we could kill her and nobody'd hardly know."

"Sure," said the girl. "And then the farmers wonder why one of their daughters have gone missing and they go looking and they find us and they say "Oh, look, bandits wintering over!" and wipe us out. Because there are *five* of us, Marten. Have you forgotten?"

"...lot more of us..." mumbled Marten, staring at his feet.

"Yes. There are. And they're currently either south lying low or they're rotting in jail because my father took it in his head to—"

She stopped and pinched the bridge of her nose. "Never mind," she said. "Never mind that. The milk is spilled, and I should stop crying over it." She took Gerta's arm. "Come with me. My name is Janna, and I suppose you're my prisoner now."

Chapter Seventeen

"No!" said Gerta. "That's—no, I'm sorry, that won't work."

Janna looked at her. She blinked a few times, slowly, and then said, "Being my prisoner isn't going to *work* for you?"

Gerta took a deep breath. "I'm sorry. I have to keep going. I'm looking for someone. He's been missing for a long time now, and—look, I didn't mean to come here. You can have my money. But I have to go."

Now that she was standing, Gerta could see that the pigeon coop was probably not where Janna and Marten were staying. There was an earth-house there, a hillock in the woods with an open doorway in one side. Piled sod on the top had sprouted grass that stuck out in tufts through the snow.

Mousebones soared in, with a flirt of wings, and landed on Gerta's shoulder. It was hard to tell in a raven, but Gerta thought that if he were a human, he would have been embarrassed.

"This is her," he said. "The girl who helped my wing. I suppose that oaf who grabbed you must have been about as well, but I didn't remember him."

Janna's eyebrows were up so far that they nearly touched her hairline. "Midnight? Is that you?"

"His name is Mousebones," said Gerta, trying to follow two conversations at once.

"I'm sorry," said the bird. "And we ravens don't apologize often, so please make a note of it. She helped my wing so I thought she'd help you. I didn't think that a human could be kind to a raven and cruel to another human."

"Mousebones," said Janna. "Well, she was called Midnight when she came flapping in here with a broken wing, and quite a job I had to set it."

"He's a he," said Gerta. "I mean—well, he's very clear that it's not my business either way, but he says that's what he'll be. Because he's not an it."

Janna stared at her.

"…um," said Gerta, who realized that she had just admitted that she heard a raven talk, which meant that Janna either thought she was lying or insane. "I mean…that is…"

I have got to stop babbling. I'm flustered, that's it. Not that anyone wouldn't *be, when they're made someone else's prisoner.*

The tips of her ears were burning now, and she was fairly sure that the blush extended most of the way to her navel.

Janna spun on her heel and snapped "Marten! Go do something useful! Make sure we've got enough firewood to last the night. It's going to be an ugly storm."

"But—"

"Go."

Marten made a long grumbling noise, like an old dog told to move, and plodded off.

"Please," said Gerta, a bit desperately, "I need to get moving before the storm hits."

Janna reached out and tucked Gerta's arm under hers. It was a companionable sort of gesture, and it also prevented Gerta from bolting into the woods. Mousebones fanned his wings to keep his balance.

"Come with me," said Janna. "You're my guest, if you prefer that to prisoner. And you can tell me all about Mousebones."

"Um…" said Gerta.

"And we'll wait out this storm that is going to land on our heads quite soon, and I will keep Marten from doing anything unpleasant, and we will even feed you. How does that sound?"

"I don't want to be any trouble…" said Gerta faintly, aware that any chance of freedom was trickling away. "Please…"

Janna smiled. Gerta had a dark suspicion that she knew exactly what she was doing. "It's no trouble at all."

Being polite is all well and good, right up until it's a trap, thought Gerta dully. *She's going to do whatever she's going to do whether I'm polite or not.*

"I suppose I could go for her eyes," said Mousebones doubtfully. "But she fixed my wing, and that would be poor payment. Um."

"It's all right," said Gerta, even though it wasn't. "Just…just stay out of reach, okay?"

Mousebones took flight and landed atop a nearby branch.

"Do you think she'll kill me?" asked Gerta, and flushed again, because Janna was standing right there beside her.

"I don't—but of course, you're asking the bird," said her captor. She shook her head and muttered "Why are the pretty ones always crazy?" half under her breath.

"I don't know," said Mousebones. "I thought I did, but I don't. Ravens know wise things, old things, and humans are a young and foolish race. I don't know." His beak gaped open and he made a small fledgling sound of distress.

"Come on, then," said Janna. "Midnight—Mousebones—can come inside as well. The ceilings are very high, and if she—he—craps on the floor, no one will notice in there." Her lips twisted.

Mousebones shook his head and fluffed up his feathers, as if something was alarming him, and then flew away. "I'll be back," he cawed. "I just—I need to think."

"Or not," said Janna, watching the raven flutter into a tree.

She led Gerta to the open doorway. Gerta felt herself resisting, trying to plant her feet, and had to concentrate to make herself stop. *If I resist, she'll drag me, and once we cross that point it will all get worse. There may be no difference between being a guest and being a prisoner, but guests are treated better. I hope.*

Janna glanced at her. "Gently," she murmured. "This charade is not all for your benefit…"

They crossed the threshold. There was a drape made of deerskin tied to one side and Janna let it down behind them.

Gerta's eyes were dazed by the shift from bright snow to darkness. She followed Janna blindly, feeling packed earth underfoot.

"Eh?" said a voice, off to her left. "Eh? What's all the fuss? Is your father home?"

"No," said Janna shortly. "Not home, and not likely to be home any time soon. The weather's turning."

"Is it?" The voice laughed, a series of short inhalations—*aah! aah! aah!*

Someone very old, thought Gerta. *A woman, I think, but very old. Older than Grandmother. Maybe older than Gran Aischa, too.*

"What have you got there, then?" asked the old woman.

"Lost traveler," said Janna. "Nothing to fret yourself over."

The voice sharpened. "Traveler? Here? Are you sure it's not a spy?"

"Quite sure." Janna was leading her away from the voice. "Don't fret yourself, Nan."

Another voice—masculine, scraped almost as thin as the first—said "If the storm runs too long, we can always eat them."

"Aah! Aah! Aah!"

Gerta's fingers closed convulsively on Janna's wrist.

"No one's eating anyone," said Janna. "We're bandits, not cannibals." Half under her breath, she muttered "An inch of snow on the ground, and the old fools always start deciding who to eat first. It's like they're looking for excuses."

Gerta thought it best not to say anything.

Her eyes were adjusting as they crossed the room. The earth house was larger than she expected, the ceiling high overhead. The beams were blackened with smoke.

The fire in the central pit was low and flickering. Radiating out from the pit, like spokes from a wheel, were a dozen sleeping areas. Most appeared unoccupied.

Seated near the fire, wrapped in blankets, were two people so old that their skin hung off them like empty sacks. It was hard to tell where flesh ended and blankets began. They looked nearly identical, but Gerta could not have said if they were related or if they were simply equally ancient.

The old woman's hands moved restlessly, working a drop-spindle, not looking down. The old man sat idle. He whispered something to his companion and they both laughed their high, gasping laughs again.

A little ways off from them, with his back to a wall, was a middle-aged man. He was sitting a little awkwardly, and it took Gerta a moment to realize that he was missing his left leg below the knee.

There was a loaded crossbow across his lap. He nodded to Janna, unsmiling, and she nodded back.

On the far side of the earthhouse was another doorway, much smaller. This one had another hide drape over it. The effect was strangely primitive, as if Gerta had stepped back in time to an age of earthen mounds and men who painted themselves in honor to the gods.

Janna herded her to the doorway. As the hide fell down behind them, Gerta heard the two old bandits begin to sing.

Chapter Eighteen

Janna's room in the earthouse was not large, but it had a hatch set in the ceiling and a long ladder up to it. Gerta's eyes fixed on that and it was hard to make herself see the rest of the room.

"I need to open it up," said Janna, following her eyes, "and knock the snow off. Have to do it every few hours or else there's six feet of snow over the hatch and I can't get into the coop."

"Coop?" said Gerta. That came out very normal, she thought. She was proud of how normal it sounded, while dread came clawing its way up her throat. She kept hearing the laugher from the other room, like birds calling over frozen ground.

"The pigeon coop," said Janna. "You go up the hatch and it's right there. It's not in great shape, but it holds pigeons. I'll show you tomorrow if you like."

"Tomorrow," said Gerta faintly. "But I must go…"

"Not until the snow is done," said Janna. "Whoever you are trying to save, they can't move any farther in this snow than you can."

"They can if they ride in the Snow Queen's sled," said Gerta.

Janna's eyebrows climbed toward her hair again. "I can see you have quite a story to tell me," she said. "And I already doubt half of it, but I shall listen quite attentively."

There was a single bed platform, very wide and covered in furs and ragged blankets. Janna sat down and patted the edge. "Have a seat," she said. "I will get you a bowl of stew and then you may tell me all this tale. I find that preposterous stories sit better on a full stomach."

"It's not preposterous," said Gerta. "Or—it is—but—" The dread was clawing at her throat again. She clenched her hands in her skirts. "It's all true. I swear it is."

"You have come here with a raven that I know personally," said Janna, "which is quite preposterous in and of itself. She—*he*— was hardly a local bird. I found him a long ways off and brought him here when it was clear that his wing needed to be set. I could just barely believe that he remembered there was food here and returned, and that you are some mad girl that follows ravens about, but that hardly seems likely either."

She smiled when she said it, and it was a good smile, a little rueful. Gerta found some tiny hope that perhaps she might yet leave alive.

I can't hope, I can't, the witch smiled too, she was very kind, kindness cannot save me...

Janna patted her arm. "It has been a long day for you," she said. "Sit and rest. I shall see to the hatch and to stew and then I will listen to what you have to say."

In the end, she told the bandit-girl everything.

She meant to omit a few things. Not so much because they were improbable, but because they were embarrassing. But one thing led to another, and one step of the journey led to the next, and she could hardly leave out the witch, after she had already told Janna that she had seen her in a dream. And if she had already explained about the witch, there was hardly anything left in the story to shame her.

"And then that man grabbed me," she finished at last. "I suppose I was trying to find you, but I didn't know—Mousebones said that you were here, but not that you were a—well—"

"A bandit?" asked Janna, amused. "Well, how would a raven know such things?"

She leaned back. "If you were trying to find us for some nefarious purpose, you'd have a better story," she said. "Or—well, no, that was an excellent story! A less improbable one, I mean."

Gerta flushed.

"And there is the matter of Mousebones…and you seeing me among wood-pigeons and grapevines." She put her chin in her hand. "That alone would make me think that you had been spying on me, but the grapevines died in the frost weeks ago and since the alternative is to believe that you have been in the woods all fall, watching me…" She shook her head slowly, chin still on her hand. "No, I think perhaps you are telling the truth as you understand it."

"As I understand it?" Gerta had calmed a good deal, between the story and the stew, enough to feel a trifle indignant about this. (The old bandits had fallen silent, which helped.)

"As you understand it," said Janna, unruffled. "You may have dreamed the parts about your Snow Queen, after all. We have only stories and your word that you were awake. You still might have come north on the strength of those dreams and run afoul of a witch and met a raven, even so."

She set aside her carved wooden bowl. The stew had been good, for an early winter stew—the deer still fat, the potatoes large. It would probably not be so good, come midwinter, when the deer were nothing but bones and hide.

"The Snow Queen is real," said Gerta, almost inaudibly.

"Many things are real," said Janna. "It does not mean that all the tales told about them are." She frowned, rubbing her hands together. "Although if it is a tale, there is one person we might ask…"

Gerta cringed when Janna lifted the hide drape and ushered her into the main room. It was very dark and smoky, and malice seemed to radiate from the two figures wrapped in furs and loosening skin.

But she followed anyway, when Janna led her across the floor, because she had no real choice. She did not want to run. Some animals would only chase you if you ran.

What am I thinking? They cannot run. I doubt they can stand without canes. They couldn't possibly chase me, not really.

Her head was aware of this. Her heart keened like a dog that remembers being beaten.

"Nan," said Janna, kneeling down an arms-length from the old woman, "you know lots of stories."

"Eh?" Nan turned her ancient head. "I do. A few."

"Tell me about the Snow Queen."

Nan inhaled. "Aah! Aah! That one I haven't heard since I was young." She turned her eyes to Gerta, who was crouched behind Janna. "Aah! Ran afoul of her, have you? She'll suck the marrow out of your bones and fill the holes with frost."

Gerta shuddered. It was not so much the threat as the gloating tone in which it was delivered.

"Never mind that," said Janna. "Tell me what you know."

"An old spirit," said Nan. "Old as old. Older than I am, but she doesn't look it."

She leaned back. Her hands never stopped on the dropspindle, spinning, spinning. The old man was asleep with his mouth open.

Gerta wrapped her arms around herself and focused on keeping Janna between them.

I don't trust you, but I trust her even less, and you don't seem to want to kill me yet...

"Old," said Nan. "I don't know much. She controls the frost, or the frost controls her, or they're the same thing. They say she made a deal with the dark powers, that love would never hurt her again." She licked her lips. "The devil took her heart and turned it cold. Now she loves however she likes, and when she's tired of them, she wraps them up in ice. She keeps them in her palace in the farthest north, they say, all the pretty boys like frozen flowers."

Kay... thought Gerta, and pictured him with ice rimed over his skin, like a snowdrop edged in frost.

"Always men?" asked Janna. "Never women?"

"Aah! Aah!" Nan paused with the dropspindle long enough to shake her finger at Janna. "Well, who's to say? No one goes to the Snow Queen's palace and lives. There might be a pretty girl or two in among the lads."

She leaned forward, peering around Janna to where Gerta hunched in silent misery. "Round little thing like her, might take the Queen awhile to freeze her out completely. She'd make a dozen meals."

"Stop it," said Janna, annoyed. "You ate a man once fifty years ago, and you relive it like it was your glory days."

"Everybody should eat somebody once," said Nan. "Changes your mind about a lot of things. Aaha!"

"We'll get no more sense out of her," said Janna, turning back to Gerta. "Come on."

"Ma'am," said Gerta, terrifying herself with her own boldness, "how does the Snow Queen travel?"

"Aah?" Nan looked up, her eyes watery. "Find your tongue at last?"

Gerta suspected that she was swaying on her feet. She thought she might throw up again.

She's only an old woman, she's only an old woman, she's not that much different than Gran Aischa, just horrible, why am I so afraid of her...?

Those awful eyes searched her face, and perhaps failed to find what they were looking for.

"Flies on the wind," said Nan, suddenly brisk. "On a sled pulled by winter weasels or some such. Never saw her, myself. Never want to. Go away, Janna, and let an old woman sleep by the fire."

Janna grabbed Gerta's wrist and pulled her back to the rear of the earthhouse.

"Winter weasels," she said. "Close enough to white otters for me. I won't swear you didn't hear the story somewhere and make up the whole mad tale, but I also won't swear it's not true."

"What's wrong with her?" asked Gerta dully.

"Old Nan? I'd say she's old, but she was like that when she was younger, too, from what I've heard. She was always cruel, but she got worse. And the healers tell me that you probably shouldn't eat your enemies, even if you're starving."

Gerta stared at her.

"Don't give me that look. I haven't eaten anyone. It doesn't come up as often as you'd think."

Gerta rubbed her forehead. It seemed that she was only plodding along from one exhaustion to the next. She was in danger here, but how was that any different than the day before, or the one before that?

Cold, cannibals, witches…it's all the same…

"Not quite as bad as all that," said Janna, which was when Gerta realized she'd been muttering to herself. *I got in the habit of talking to myself on the road. I have to stop if I'm going to be around people.* She pressed her lips together.

"We've got the cannibals, certainly," said Janna, "but no witches, and we'll be warm enough tonight."

Janna surprised her by springing up the ladder on the wall, and flipping open the hatch. A dusting of snow came down around them.

She banged the hatch a few times, letting a cold draft into the lodge, then shut it again. Gerta shivered.

"That'll do for the night," said the bandit girl. "Now I'm going to bed, and I suggest you do the same. Unless you'd like to get in the sauna…no?"

Gerta glanced around, wondering where she was going to sleep.

"It's large enough for two," said Janna, "and will warm up faster. Here." She opened a trunk and tossed Gerta a piece of fabric.

It was a nightshirt. It was pale blue and embroidered with little flowers around the hem. It did not look even remotely like something that Janna herself would wear.

It was also about two sizes too large and hung on Gerta like a tent. "Did you...err...make this?" asked Gerta.

"All stolen goods, I'm afraid," said Janna.

Gerta blinked. *Well, of course, they're bandits...did I think she was spending her nights with an embroidery hoop?*

Janna nobly refrained from laughing at her, and simply pulled back the furs. She had changed into her own nightclothes, which had significantly less embroidery.

"Come on," she said. "We're stuck in here for a few days, and the more time we spend asleep, the less time we spend going for each other's throats, or listening to Nan talk about who to eat first."

The sleeping platform was larger than Gerta's trundlebed, larger even than her grandmother's big four-poster. Gerta crept in, staying close to one side, as far from Janna as possible.

What do I expect her to do? Strangle me in my sleep?

She had no idea.

Janna pushed a pillow in her direction and rolled over. Her hair, freed from the kerchief, was thick and dark and curly.

"If you're thinking of waiting until I fall asleep and sneaking out, by the way," she said in a conversational tone, "I'd warn you that Aaron—the one with the crossbow—doesn't sleep well. He'll be awake for most of the night, and if he is asleep, one footstep out of place will wake him up. The first shot will probably be to wound, but you never know his mood."

Gerta stared at her back, wide-eyed.

"Sleep well," said Janna, turning down the lamp. "I'll be interested to hear about your dreams."

Chapter Nineteen

Gerta dreamed that night of rowan trees, of long roots that twined around her. The rowans, too, were dreaming under the blanket of snow. Squirrels scratched around the base of the trees and woodpeckers were tucked into holes drilled into the heartwood. The trees dreamed of these things, of the movement of carpenter worms in wood and the caterpillars sleeping in hollowed out twigs.

She felt very large, immense, stretching out in all directions. Large and cold, alive but dormant.

Nothing happened in the great forest except the fall of snow. Gerta stood in the heart of the rowan and watched the snow pile up and waited for the sap to rise.

Then a disturbance—a chiming sound and a howl of wind— and the trees shuddered. In their hollow nests, the woodpeckers huddled together. The squirrels chattered worriedly in their drays. Only the caterpillars seemed unbothered. Very few things bother a caterpillar.

The wind passed. The trees slipped into a deeper sleep and the small animals settled. The Snow Queen's sled had passed, and was gone into the distance.

She woke very late. Janna prodded her shoulder and said "I've got to go check on the wood-pigeons. Do you want to come with me, or sleep some more?"

Gerta blinked muzzily up at her. For a moment all that she could think was that she was in the room with this strange, familiar girl and they clearly knew each other, and perhaps they were friends.

Janna handed her a cup of tea.

Gerta's head cleared. She looked toward the doorway and the hide drape, and remembered Nan and Aaron with the crossbow. She was a prisoner. She took a drink, hoping that hot tea would fill up the spaces in her that would otherwise be filling with despair.

"I'll come with you," she said. Part of her wanted to go back to the peacefulness of the rowan dream, to sleep away as much of her captivity as possible, but the wood-pigeons would be outside. Outside was closer to freedom than inside.

And I might see Mousebones again.

She pulled on her clothes under the nightgown. Janna watched, looking faintly amused, and Gerta flushed for no particular reason. *I know I'm plump and pasty and I look weak. She doesn't need to look at me like that.*

When she was dressed, Janna went up the ladder again. She flipped the hatch back—more snow fell inside—and climbed the rest of the way out. "Come on," she called down. "It's not warm, but the snow's let up."

Gerta went up the ladder slowly and poked her head out at the top. Janna put down a hand and pulled her out onto the roof of the earthlodge.

The world was blinding, dazzling white. The sun blazed off the snow crystals. Gerta shaded her eyes and blinked away red spots.

Mousebones landed on the snow next to her, looking like a black paper cut-out against the snow.

"Aurk! Are you hurt? Did the humans pick at you?"

"Only a little," said Gerta. "At least, for now."

"Arrk!"

Janna shook her head. "I admit, I'm starting to believe that you do talk to him."

"It's easy to prove," said Gerta, a bit nettled. "Hold up your fingers behind your back."

Janna raised her eyebrow, but put her hands behind her back. "And now…?"

"Mousebones, can you tell me how many she's holding up?"

The raven made a grumpy noise. "I'm not a circus animal, you know."

"Please? It'll make my life easier."

"Arrrkk…" The raven hopped around behind Janna. "Two."

"Two," said Gerta.

Janna's eyebrows went up. Her hands moved a bit. "How many now?"

"Four," reported Mousebones. Gerta passed this on.

"How many now?"

The raven took off, cawing irritably.

"Um. He says he's not doing this any more. If you won't listen to another human tell you the truth, you're an…addled egg that shouldn't hatch."

The sound of Janna's laughter was loud and exuberant, even through the muffling effect of the snow. "Does he, now? That's the sort of thing I'd expect. He used to peck at me when I tried to check on his wing."

She put her hands on her knees and leaned forward. "Well. I suppose I am obliged to believe that either you are telling the truth, or you are some kind of witch, and I do not believe that a witch would let herself be caught so easily. So. You can speak to ravens. Interesting."

"One raven anyway," said Gerta. "I haven't tried any of the others." Janna laughed again.

The pigeon coop looked to be half falling down, but the door was solid in its frame. Janna scraped aside the snow blocking it with her boot and pushed it inward.

Soft cooing greeted her, and a grunt that definitely did not come from a pigeon.

Gerta followed her inside.

Perches ran across the wall on one side. Birds lined it, fluffed up and cooing. Those highest up were silent and still.

On the other side, there were no perches. Instead there was a reindeer.

Gerta stared.

It was old. She could see that, even knowing nothing of reindeer. The bones of its face were fine and sharp, the skin stretched tight over them. Its muzzle was white and its eyes were cloudy.

"Rescued him from a trader," said Janna shortly. "He's too old to haul a load like he used to, but the damn fool was beating him. By the time we were done, all that man's goods would fit in a backpack he could carry himself." She smiled grimly.

"Good," said Gerta, and was surprised at her own anger. "*Good.*"

She crouched down and offered the reindeer her hand, as if it were a strange dog. The animal looked at her with its filmy eyes, then stretched out its neck. It breathed gently into the palm of her hand.

Janna cursed. Gerta looked up, startled.

"Frozen," said the other girl grimly. "Right on the perches. Oh, damn. I thought it would be warm enough. It's always *been* warm enough. What happened?"

She stroked one of the silent birds on the top perch, and Gerta saw that it was dead.

The Snow Queen happened, thought Gerta. *My dream last night. The Snow Queen passed over, and froze them.*

She did not wish to say this right now. She scratched the reindeer's forehead instead, and it sighed.

There were four dead birds, and two that were stupefied with cold. Janna took the dead ones down and set them on their backs in the snow outside the door. The other pigeons cooed and flapped their wings. The dazed ones sat in silent, stupid misery.

Janna crouched over the two injured ones, frowning. When she stretched their wings out, they shed feathers from wings patched white with frost.

"What a mess," she muttered. "I can't fix this."

"Where do they come from?" asked Gerta.

"I find them, mostly," said Janna. "Sometimes traders carry them. There's good eating on a pigeon, and they'll last in a cage for awhile. But mostly they fall out of trees and I pick them up. They're not bright."

"What will you do with them?" asked Gerta. "Will you kill them?"

"Kill them?" Janna looked surprised, then amused. A smile crossed her lips as she looked at Gerta. It was not entirely kind.

She stood up and took a step forward, then another. Gerta backed away, suddenly nervous, but the coop was small and there was a doorframe in her back.

Janna was taller than she was, a good deal taller. Taller than Kay, it occurred to her. Gerta had to look up to meet the robber girl's eyes.

"What you're really asking," said Janna, her voice quite gentle, "is will I kill *you?*"

Gerta swallowed hard.

Janna tilted her head. She was standing very close. Gerta could feel the doorframe digging into her shoulder, the metal bolt against her back.

She's waiting for an answer. Don't look scared. Don't look scared.

Bit late for that, isn't it?

Gerta licked her lips. They felt very dry. "Yes," she said. "That's what I'm asking."

Janna kissed her.

Gerta's eyes went very wide.

But girls don't—not with other girls—

Well.

Apparently they did.

This was not like kissing Kay behind the stove. This was not even remotely close to it. Janna's hand slid up the back of her neck and drew her face up. Her mouth was hot, not cold. Her fingers were warm and strong.

Kay hadn't touched her at all.

Somewhat dazed, Gerta thought, *Am I supposed to be doing something with my lips—?*

The thought was not even half completed. Janna's tongue flicked over her lips, coaxed them open. There were no more thoughts. She had never felt anything like that. She was aware that she was shaking. Her chest felt as if it were melting—was she holding her breath? Who could breathe?

They broke apart and Gerta gasped for air.

Janna chuckled.

They were close enough, breast to breast, that Gerta could feel the laugh as much as hear it. She stared at Janna's collarbone, much too shocked to look in her eyes. There was a pulse in her head and between her legs and she could not seem to get enough air.

Janna slipped her fingers under Gerta's chin and lifted it. Her thumb stroked the corner of Gerta's mouth.

She turned her head, just a little, into the caress—then realized what she was doing.

She just—we just—

Her cheeks burned with sudden mortification.

"Oh dear," said Janna softly, while Gerta cursed the pale skin that made her blushes so obvious. *I bet you can't tell when she's embarrassed.*

It was almost impossible to imagine Janna being embarrassed by anything.

The robber girl let her go. Her smile was secret, sardonic, kind.

"Sometimes I kill them," she said. "If they can't be healed. If they can't stop attacking the others." She stepped back. "But mostly I let them go. Eventually."

She walked out of the coop and it was several minutes before Gerta could summon the composure to follow her.

Chapter Twenty

It was a short winter day and absolutely nothing happened. Gerta stayed out of the way of Nan. Janna needed help dragging hay in for the reindeer, so she did that.

The snow, when she tested it, was deep. The trees all looked the same. If Mousebones was her guide, she might make it out, but she would be cold and floundering and would leave a trail that a blind man could follow.

Do I leave? Do I dare? I can't run. I have to get Janna to let me go. The kiss burned in her memory like a brand.

Surely...surely... She did not even know what she was thinking. Her mind was tossing up nonsense phrases.

She dragged hay from an outbuilding, armload after armload. She was fairly certain that she blushed whenever Janna looked at her.

She's the one who did it! I don't know why I'm the one who's embarrassed!

Because you enjoyed it, and you weren't thinking about Kay at all, said a traitorous part of her mind.

If she could have buried that part in the snow, she would have.

Marten glared at her from across the yard. Gerta ducked her head and pretended not to see.

That night, when they crawled into the same bed, Gerta's heart thrummed in her chest like a nervous bird.

Will she kiss me again?

She shivered at the thought.

The act of pulling on her nightclothes was suddenly fraught. She caught a glimpse of Janna's lean, scarred body in the mirror and turned away, feeling pasty and wobbly by comparison. She blushed again, for no good reason, and yanked her clothes over her head.

When she had her arms through the proper holes and her hair out of her face, Janna was smiling at her, and that made her shiver again, for reasons she couldn't even begin to explain.

"Cold?" asked Janna. "Get under the covers. It'll warm up."

It was easier to nod. Cold. Yes. Not shaking hard for some other reason that felt like fear and Christmas morning wrapped up together.

Will she?

They lay down. Janna rolled over and snuggled her back against Gerta's side. She was very warm and very solid.

She could roll over any minute. She could put her mouth over mine again...

...I wouldn't mind.

She blushed again, grateful that Janna couldn't see her face. What was wrong with her? Girls didn't kiss other girls, or at least, not like that. *Boys* kissed girls like that.

Well, in theory.

Kay didn't. I don't think he knew how.

In fairy tales, it was the kiss that woke the sleeping maiden. After her only experience with kissing, Gerta had been skeptical about that, but she certainly wasn't now. A kiss like Janna's could have brought back the dead. Corpses three days old would hop off the pyre if someone kissed them like that.

There were always warnings in town, about nice girls not letting boys do too much before they married. Gerta's grandmother had muttered about that a time or two, once Gerta was old enough to wear a proper bodice.

Nobody ever mentioned that you didn't let *girls* kiss you. It had never even occurred to her that was an option.

Having now occurred to her, she couldn't think of any reason it shouldn't be an option…and then she thought of at least three houses in the village where two women lived together and felt a rush of embarrassment for having been so incredibly *dim*.

"What will you do?" asked Janna.

"W…what?" Gerta felt slow and stupid.

The robber girl looked over her shoulder in the dim light. "When you find your friend. And the Snow Queen."

"Oh!" Gerta struggled to think. *Yes. Kay. Yes.* "I don't know. I suppose I'll see if there's some way to sneak him out."

"And if she catches you?"

Gerta shrugged. "I don't know. I guess…I guess I'll try to stop her."

"Stab her with your little kitchen knife, will you?" asked Janna, rolling over on her back.

"If I have to," said Gerta.

Janna laughed again, ruefully, and shook her head. "I believe you would. I suppose you'll get killed, if no one goes along with you."

"I've done all right," said Gerta indignantly. "I got this far, didn't I?"

"Yes, and walked into a bandit camp like a fuzzy little chick into a fox's den."

Gerta flushed again.

She opened her mouth to say that it had been Mousebones's fault and she'd certainly know what to look for in the future, and Janna propped herself up on one elbow and kissed her again.

It was slower this time, more languid, just as deep. Janna tasted like woodsmoke and cinnamon tea. When Gerta came up for air, gasping like a drowning woman, Janna did not stop but moved her lips slowly down the other girl's jaw, up to her ear.

"You could get into a great deal of trouble alone," she breathed.

Gerta trembled like a leaf in a gale, surprised her teeth weren't chattering. "Yes," she said finally—an agreement, an encouragement, she had no idea at all. "*Yes.*"

"Of course," murmured the robber girl, "you could get into a great deal *more* trouble with me." She trailed a fingertip over the edge of Gerta's ear. "Go to sleep. Tomorrow we'll see about getting you out of the fox's den."

"And how," said Gerta, surprised at herself, "am I supposed to get to sleep after that?"

Janna threw back her head and laughed. "Perhaps you really would stab the Snow Queen after all."

She bent over—Gerta tensed—but she only pressed a chaste kiss to Gerta's forehead and rolled over.

And apparently went to sleep.

Gerta let out a long, wavering sigh. Her body felt drawn agonizingly tight.

Is she going to let me go?

That's…that's a good thing. I'll get away from the robbers. That's good.

I'll be able to go after Kay.

Kay. Right.

Him.

Right.

Staring into the dark, her skin seemed to burn in the place where Janna had touched her.

Chapter Twenty-One

They went the next morning to feed the pigeons. Gerta felt her stomach lurch whenever Janna came near her, but the bandit girl seemed to realize this and left space between them wherever they stood.

The message—if it was a message—seemed clear. If she wanted the distance between them crossed, Gerta would have to be the one to cross it.

I'm leaving, though. I don't have to do anything. I just...I can leave. Yes.

One of the injured pigeons had died. Janna sighed, cradling the cold body in her hands.

"It was the Snow Queen," said Gerta.

Janna glanced up at her, raising an eyebrow.

"She passed overhead," said Gerta. Did the other girl believe her? She wasn't sure. "Two days ago. In the rowan dream, I saw—" She put her hands to her face, feeling her cheeks heating under her fingers.

"You didn't say anything," said Janna.

"I didn't think you'd believe me," said Gerta. "I know how it sounds. I dream about trees and the trees saw a frost spirit and by the way it's the one who stole my friend away." Her laugh rang thin and wild in her own ears. "I know it's mad. But that was what I saw."

Janna sighed. "I said that I believed you," she said. "And you may be foolish enough to walk into a robber's den, but I think you'd come up with a better story than that." She stared down at the dead bird in her hands, brooding.

Mousebones landed in the doorway with a flirt of wings. "Ark!"

"Mousebones!"

"Ark. You're alive, yet. And so am I, and so is she, so I suppose that's something." The raven picked at one of his feet with his beak. "Is she going to eat that pigeon?"

"He'd like the pigeon," said Gerta. "Um." It felt strange to ask that. "You don't have to. I don't think he'll starve."

"I might," said Mousebones, aggrieved. "It's not like someone's leaving eyeballs out in the snow for any hungry raven that might come by."

"He can have it," said Janna. "Someone might as well get a little good out of it." She approached the doorway and set the dead pigeon down in the snow to one side of the door, where they would not need to see the raven picking at it.

"Did you mean it?" asked Gerta. "About letting me leave?"

"Yes," said Janna. "Though I'm still working out the details. I am not planning on staying here myself, you understand. But Marten and Old Nan won't be happy to see me go, and Aaron will not be best pleased either."

"Aaron?"

"With the crossbow. A friend of my father's." She stood up. Outside the door, Mousebones tore at the frozen pigeon.

"In theory, I am in charge here until my father comes back," Janna said, "but I believe he's been hanged. And since it is only fear of my father that is keeping Marten from throwing his weight around, that will make things difficult for me sooner rather than later."

Her father's been hanged. And she doesn't sound like she cares at all. Gerta was not sure if Janna's indifference impressed her or frightened her.

Then again, he must be a bandit chief, so he's probably not a nice man...

"Aaron fears I'll get myself into trouble going off," Janna continued. "But staying up here with a restless bully and a pair of old cannibals is not my idea of pleasure. Nan knows I'm bringing in most of the food, and Marten's got a fool notion that if he is ruling the roost, I'll swoon at his feet, so no one's keen to see me haring off into the woods."

The notion of Janna swooning at anyone's feet boggled Gerta's imagination.

"So we shall have to find a way to leave quietly," said Janna. "And get a long way away."

"I have to go north," said Gerta. "To the Snow Queen's palace. She's got Kay there." Nan's story of frozen boys in the palace made of ice haunted her thoughts, as hard as she tried to forget it.

Was Kay in there already? Would she get there and find him as hard as stone, with a rime of ice over his frost blue eyes? "I have to get there before she freezes him."

"And you don't know where it is," said Janna. "Or even if there are directions mere mortals can follow." She shook her head.

"I've come this far," said Gerta. "I have to try."

Janna looked like she was about to say something else, but there was a grumbling, creaking noise from the far side of the shed.

The ancient reindeer in the corner heaved himself to his feet.

Gerta jumped back, startled. Janna took a step back and laughed. "My goodness! I thought you were looking like dying, old man."

The reindeer stood, swaying. His legs looked very thin beneath him.

He opened his mouth and breathed out, his breath barely frosting the air, making a noise so low that Gerta could hardly hear it.

"He *is* dying," said Mousebones, from the doorway. The bird cocked his head. "He says…You must walk the reindeer road, if you are going to the farthest North. He would take you but he cannot. His bones are full of frost, he says."

Gerta, not taking her eyes off the reindeer, translated for Janna.

"The reindeer road," said Janna. "Up north? With the reindeer people?"

"Yes," said Mousebones. "No. What? Make up your mind, mammal! Ark!"

The reindeer wheezed gently, and Gerta thought it sounded like laughter.

"There are many roads," translated the raven. "Some the reindeer walk with humans, and some they walk alone. He would take you if he could, but he cannot. So you must walk the reindeer road instead. He will give you this, because the human was kind to him."

"I wouldn't have left him to that trader," said Janna, when she heard this. "But how do we walk the reindeer road, then?"

Mousebones cocked his head, listening but not speaking.

After a moment he began to laugh.

"You will not like this, Gerta. Aurk! Aurk! Aurk!"

Chapter Twenty-Two

"No," said Gerta. "Absolutely not! It's horrible! I won't let you!"

Janna rubbed her face. "I have to believe that was Mousebones," she said. "It would take a raven to come up with something that revolting."

Mousebones looked proud and a bit smug.

The reindeer laughed his soft, wheezing laugh again.

"Humans are so touchy about skin," translated Mousebones. "It is only a shape. My soul will go on to the herd of stars, and then when I am tired of stars, into the young calves that sleep in their mother's bellies. I will die soon anyway. Let me give you a gift, for kindness's sake."

"But to cut off his skin and *wear* it?" Gerta felt ill. She could imagine how the inside of the skin would feel. *Raw and bloody and squishy. I'd be inside a horrible bloody tent.*

"It will let you walk the reindeer road, he says," said Mousebones. "And—ah—" He tilted his head, listening. "Oh. Hmm."

"Thirdhand conversations are maddening," said Janna, to no one in particular.

"He says that it's too hot down here in this country," said Gerta bleakly. "He wants his skin to lie somewhere cold, where a reindeer can be comfortable for more than one season a year. He will be a spirit, but even a spirit likes to know that his old home is well-cared for."

"Sounds fair," said Janna practically. "I can skin him, if you like."

Gerta gave her a shocked look. "But he's not dead!"

"I can do that, too, if it's really what he wants."

Gerta put her face in her hands.

The reindeer took a few steps forward and rested his muzzle on Janna's arm. She looked down into his eyes.

"Yes," she said after a minute. "I believe it is."

"No!" said Gerta. "He can't—I mean—not for *me*. Nobody dies for me!"

Janna rubbed the reindeer behind the ears. "Are you willing to die for your little friend the Queen took?"

"Yes." Gerta raked her hands through her hair. "But it's different. He doesn't even know Kay. And I mean—it's *Kay*. I'm just me. It doesn't matter if *I* do it."

Janna's eyes narrowed, and Gerta had a strong feeling that the other girl was angry. But she kept stroking the reindeer behind the ears and said nothing.

Mousebones flapped a bit. "Can I have your eyes?" he asked the reindeer.

"Mousebones!"

"What? He's not going to be using them."

The reindeer snorted.

"There's got to be another way," said Gerta hopelessly. "Where nobody has to die."

The raven rippled his wings in a shrug. "Maybe the human flock coming knows one."

"What?" Janna's head shot up.

"The human flock," said Mousebones. "From the south."

It occurred to Gerta belatedly that she shouldn't have translated that. If someone was coming to rescue her, she'd have had a better chance to get away if Janna didn't know about it.

Except she's going to let me go. And I know she said she'd go with me, but I could get away, or convince her to leave—but how do I get to the far north, then? I'd have to walk through the snow...

...unless I walked the reindeer road.

It was utterly mad. She didn't even know how it would work. Put on a bloody reindeer hide and start walking?

It is mad. It's as mad as a woman coming in a sled pulled by otters to steal your friend, and as mad as a talking raven and dreams of plants that come true.

"What sort of men?" Janna demanded. "Guards? Bandits? Who?"

Mousebones fluffed his feathers up in a shrug. "All humans look alike, he says," said Gerta. "They have swords and a pack horse. The pack horse has seen better days."

"How far away?"

"They were leaving the road and going into the forest when he was flying around in the morning."

Janna cursed. "Why didn't you tell us before?"

Mousebones looked blank. "It's a human flock. It's not *my* flock."

"Is it guards?" asked Gerta.

"If we're lucky," said Janna grimly. "If we're not, it's my father coming home. Either way, we need to get out of here."

She doesn't want her father to come home?

Janna began going down the line of birds, picking them up one at a time and thrusting them into a wicker cage. They chirped grumpily, but did not seem to mind, and Janna's hands were gentle despite her speed.

"What's wrong?" asked Gerta. She wanted to help—but then again, maybe she should be trying to stall Janna—but—

"They'll realize that Taggen's not here," said Janna. "And then Aaron and the oldsters will realize that Taggen's not down south with them. And that's a conversation I'd rather not have." She handed Gerta the cage full of pigeons.

"Who's Taggen?" asked Gerta. The cage wasn't heavy, but she could feel them moving around and occasionally soft wings or hard feet would brush her skin.

"A boorish young bastard that my father left in charge. I might possibly have killed him. Come on, old man, let's get you outside…" She took the reindeer's lead rope and began to coax him along.

Gerta gaped at her. "You *killed* someone?"

Why am I surprised? I shouldn't be surprised. It's stupid to be surprised about this, I knew she was violent, I knew it and I let her kiss me anyway—I mean, not really let, but I didn't mind, and I should have because she's killed people and it should have been different.

"Somebody was bound to do it and it just happened to be me. Men like Taggen are born for killing. Come on!"

Janna led the reindeer out into the snow and down the back of the hill. Gerta followed with her arms full of doves.

"Wait here," said Janna, handing her the lead rope for the reindeer. She scrambled back up the hill and down the ladder.

It occurred to Gerta that she could run right now, and be rid of both the oncoming men and Janna the killer. But her arms were full of birds and she was holding the reindeer and probably she could drop both and run but there was snow everywhere and her tracks would be obvious and Janna was probably going to be faster than she was and then they'd have to have the awkward conversation where Gerta admitted that she'd tried to escape, and…well.

The pigeons might freeze.

And she's killed people. And I don't have any reason to think she wouldn't kill me.

Janna reappeared from the hilltop and slid down the embankment. She was carrying two packs and a cloak over her arm.

"All right," she said. "Let's get the birds on the reindeer's back. Ah—can you ask Mousebones to ask him if he can make it a few miles?"

Mousebones dutifully relayed this.

"The frost is nearly at my heart," said the reindeer, "but there are a few more strides left in me, at least."

Gerta wasn't sure if this was a yes or a no, but Janna nodded.

"Good," she said, and took the lead. "Let's—"

"Where do you think you're going?" asked Marten.

Chapter
Twenty-Three

Gerta closed her teeth on a frightened squeak—*don't give yourself away*—and clutched the cage closer to her chest.

Janna turned toward Marten, looking disdainful. "I'm going to release the pigeons."

The big man looked at her, then over at Gerta and the cage. Gerta tried to look like a person who was releasing pigeons, not a person who was escaping. She wasn't sure what the difference was.

Marten stared at the doves for a few minutes, then back over at Janna. "So open the cage."

"Not here," said Janna, annoyed. "And have Aaron shoot one for supper tonight, after I went to all that work saving it? I'll take them out in the woods. I don't mind eating pigeon, but I'm not eating friends."

"Why you got the girl, then?"

"God's teeth!" said Janna. "Because somebody's got to keep an eye on her, and those old cannibals will have her in the pot before you can turn around. And I don't much trust you, either."

Marten grunted. For a moment—only a moment—Gerta thought she might have gotten away with it. Marten was clearly a stupid man.

But her grandmother had said once, "It's surprisingly hard to fool very stupid people." So Gerta watched him with her heart in her throat, even as Janna rolled her eyes and tugged the reindeer's lead.

Marten's face darkened.

"You got packs," he said. "You got packs and you don't need packs to let birds go. And you've got her, and you're going somewhere."

He reached out and grabbed Janna's arm.

"Get your hands off me!" snapped Janna, trying to yank away.

"No," said Marten. "You aren't going away. You'll stay here."

"I said, get your hands off me! My father left in me in charge!"

Marten shook his head and began pulling her around the edge of the hill, toward the entrance to the mound.

Janna went for her knife.

If he had been holding her other arm, it might have worked. But she had to draw awkwardly with her left and he saw her do it.

"None of that!" said Marten, and punched her in the side of the head.

Gerta gasped.

It was suddenly, shockingly violent. It sounded like someone dropping a sack of flour on a board. Janna's head snapped back and she staggered and went to her knees.

"No!" said Gerta. "No, stop!"

Marten pulled Janna up. She stumbled in his wake, her face slack and dazed.

"Stop!" Gerta ran after them, her arms still full of pigeons. Her voice was a thin, useless bleat. What was she going to do? Attack Marten? Get hit herself? "Stop! Please!"

He didn't.

Mousebones dropped out of the trees, cawing corvine obscenities, and tore at Marten's scalp. Marten slapped at the raven with his free hand.

"Damn bird!"

"Stop!" cried Gerta. Her voice was not loud enough, nobody could hear her, why couldn't she shout loud enough to make someone listen? Mousebones was going to get hurt. If Marten hit him like he'd hit Janna, the raven's delicate skeleton would shatter into a thousand pieces.

Mousebones broke away and swooped upward. His scarred wing was beating hard and Gerta couldn't tell if he was cursing it or Marten.

All three of them broke through the trees, into the clearing. Janna was trying to pull away, shaking her head now like a horse with flies. "Let go," she mumbled. "Hands...hands...off..."

Gerta caught up with them. She clutched the cage with one hand and grabbed for Janna's arm with the other. "Let her go!"

Marten turned back. Janna half-staggered, half-fell against him, and tried to elbow him in the ribs as she went.

He lifted his hand to strike her again and an arrow sprouted out of his neck.

Gerta stared.

Her first response was not shock or horror or dismay, but only bafflement. Why were there feathers coming out of his neck? What was going on?

The moment stretched and stretched and very slowly Gerta thought *it's an arrow* and then *there is an arrow sticking in him* and then *people who have arrows in them die* and then Marten opened his mouth and blood came out and he fell.

Gerta stumbled backward, but she was not thinking clearly enough to let go of Janna, so she pulled the older girl back with her. Janna was not exactly walking but she could stumble.

Gerta would have kept backing up for hours, possibly forever, but she ran into something hot and solid and staggered.

The reindeer went *Hwuff!*

In the doorway of the earthhouse, Aaron lowered his crossbow.

They stood there. Gerta breathed and the reindeer breathed and Janna breathed and Marten would never breathe again. From inside, very faintly, Gerta could hear Old Nan calling, "What is it? Who'd you get?"

Janna leaned heavily on Gerta's shoulder. "I'm all right," she croaked finally. "I'm all right."

"You don't sound all right," whispered Gerta, looking nervously toward Aaron.

Janna followed her gaze. She, too, looked to Aaron. And then, with unsteady grace, she bowed to the man with the crossbow.

Aaron nodded, once, and turned away.

Mousebones landed on the reindeer's antlers and said "The man-flock is coming this way. They cut right through the trees like they knew where they were going."

"We have to go," said Janna. "Fast."

It was easier said than done. Janna could walk, with difficulty. Three steps would be fine and the fourth would be set a little too wide. Gerta had to hold her arm to help steer her, and trust to Mousebones and the reindeer to lead the way.

"He didn't hit me that hard," said Janna, sounding as if she were trying to convince herself. "I'm not seeing double. It's just my eye."

Her eye was already swelling closed. She held snow against the side of her head, and that seemed to help, but her steps were still uneven.

"Okay," said Gerta, holding her by the elbow. "Why did Aaron let us go?"

"Because he'd have to shoot me otherwise and he knows it."

The reindeer carried their packs. His tendons clacked at every step, a hollow sound like fingers snapping. His hooves cut through the snow like knives, every step precise. Gerta tried to walk in the holes he left behind.

"We're leaving a trail," said Janna. She turned her head carefully, holding her chin exactly level, and looked behind them. The muscles under Gerta's fingers tightened. "Anyone could follow that."

"Will they?" asked Gerta.

"When they get to the lodge and find Marten dead? Yes."

"What do we do?"

"I don't know."

"You will walk the reindeer road," said Mousebones. "He says, anyway. I'd listen, if I were you."

"Will it work?" asked Gerta. "I mean—if we take his skin—will that really work?"

"Aurk!" Mousebones flapped. "Don't ask a raven. Reindeer know reindeer best. If he says it will, why wouldn't it? There's enough magic stuck to you that a skin could stick, too."

They floundered on in the reindeer's wake. It had been less than an hour since the reindeer suggested taking his hide.

And I was horrified and now I am probably going to try it.

She tried to feel something about this. She could not. Her feelings seemed to be lying back in the clearing, as throat-shot as Marten.

If this is what I do to get away, then I will do it. Someone will have to help me.

Janna took a few deep breaths and straightened. "I'll need half an hour," she said. "It'd be less, but I'm not moving well right now." Gerta nodded.

The reindeer walked a little way farther, his great head turning from side to side. Then he seemed to see something that he liked, and turned.

"Here," he said, through Mousebones. "Here is a good place. If my bones lie here, I will not mind the heat."

The snow here lay over thickets of waxy-leaved evergreen shrubs. A rowan tree, limbs bare, stood among the firs. A human would have overlooked it, but perhaps a deer might find it beautiful.

Janna leaned against a tree, breathing deeply. "All right," she said. "Are you sure?"

The reindeer stepped up to her and tilted his head back.

Janna could not nod, but she let out a little huff of breath. "Very well."

It was happening too fast. She knew she would do it, but she had just seen a man die and she was about to see a reindeer die, and—"Wait!" said Gerta.

The reindeer rolled a mild eye in her direction.

"You have no time," said Mousebones, overhead.

Gerta wrapped her arms around the reindeer's neck and said "Thank you." Tears were pouring down her face. Where had they come from? *I don't have time to cry, I have to help Janna, I can't do this—*

"It will be well," translated Mousebones. "Strike, human, and cut the frost from my heart at last."

Janna put her hand on the reindeer's chin and pressed her forehead against his muzzle for only a moment. It came to Gerta that the other girl had known him for far longer and loved him in her own way and she cried then for Janna's grief.

The knife was sharp and silver. The blood was boiling red.

The reindeer sank to his knees and Janna sank down with him, her clothes soaked in scarlet. She held his head while he breathed his last and then she stood. Her one good eye was bright with unshed tears.

"This is all quite mad," she said hoarsely. "I am listening to a girl talk for a raven. My father is coming and now he will kill me if he can. But I don't know what else there is to do. Help me roll him over."

Mousebones circled the clearing on dark wings. Gerta took a stumbling step forward, then another, and helped Janna skin the reindeer who had been her friend.

Chapter Twenty-Four

It was hard, messy work, and in very short order it was hard and messy and cold.

The reindeer's body was hot and the hide was warm, but the blood cooled on Gerta's hands and she knelt in bloody slush that refroze around her legs.

If there was magic here, it was nothing Gerta recognized. The Snow Queen's magic was cold and clean and pure. The witch's had been drowsy and sweet.

This was mud and hide and horror. Gerta had never skinned a large animal. Her grandmother got meat from the butcher, already separated. She'd skinned rabbits before, and plucked chickens, but there was a vast difference between a rabbit and a reindeer.

Janna had skinned deer. Her movements were deft, even one-eyed and groggy. There was only one knife between them, so all Gerta could do was grab things when Janna told her to, and try not to look at the dead reindeer's face.

How is this even going to work? I don't know how to do magic! Do I put the hide on…or am I supposed to do something…say something…

Did we just kill him for nothing?

Her heart clenched thinking of this, but all she had to do was hold a leg up out of the way while Janna slit down the belly, so it didn't matter if she couldn't see for tears.

"Do I leave the head?" asked Janna.

"I don't know," said Gerta. "I've never done this before."

126

"I don't know if anyone's done this before. Where's Mousebones?"

Gerta shook her head. The raven had vanished.

Maybe it's just as well. If he was trying to eat the poor reindeer's eyes, I don't think I could handle it.

"I'll leave the head, then. It takes longer, that's all, since I have to skin backward." She grimaced "If we could get the head up in a tree, this'd be easier, but I don't think either of us can lift him."

They tried. They couldn't. It seemed obscene to be manhandling the reindeer's body like that. They laid him back down and slumped against each other, shoulder to shoulder. Janna's breathing was harsh and steamed against the air.

It was nearly twenty minutes later that Mousebones returned. He landed in the snow and cocked his head.

"The man-flock's arrived at your old nest."

"What are they doing?"

"Oh, it's a regular anthill. Lot of swirling and shouting and people carrying things back and forth." He fixed an eye on Janna. "A few of them are coming up your backtrail."

Janna started to nod, then grimaced. Blood smudged her cheekbones, mostly the reindeer's, a little of her own.

"I'm working as fast as I can," she said. She had her hands under the reindeer's skin now, punching at it to pull it away from the body.

"What do we do once it's off?" asked Gerta desperately. "Are we—are we supposed to do something?"

"Awk! You put it on."

Janna had all but the front legs clear now, cutting off the hide at the joint. The skinned body was red and white, garishly bright against the snow. Gerta tried not to look at it and hated herself for not wanting to look.

That's the reindeer. Part of him, anyway.

She shoved her hair out of her face with a bloody hand. *And how will it do him any good if I stare at what's left of him and feel sick?*

Someone shouted off in the distance. Gerta jerked upright, looking over the bushes, then realized that was a very stupid thing to do and dropped down beside Janna.

"Almost," panted the bandit girl. "I hope holes don't matter." She gave a final pull, nearly tearing the skin off, cutting the last bits holding flesh to hide—and it was free.

More shouting. Whether they were bandits or soldiers no longer seemed remotely important.

Janna clutched the hide to her chest. It was pale underneath, stained pink with blood. "Ready?" she panted.

"Yes? I don't know!" Gerta laughed, because things had gone too far for tears. "How do you get ready for this? What if it doesn't work? Are we supposed to say some kind of words?"

Mousebones looked at her—a little oddly, Gerta thought.

"Try *thank you*," he said, and then Janna dropped the hide over her shoulders.

Gerta did not have time to fear that it wasn't working. All she felt was the clammy interior of the hide, and the weight of the skull, bowing her shoulders.

The weight bowed her right down to the ground. Her hands hit the snow and a shock traveled up her arms.

She was still cold, but the hide was warm. It wrapped around her like love, like her grandmother hugging her, and then *she* was warm and everything was warm and something happened to her spine and her legs and she gasped in surprise and it came out as *Hwufff!*

"Holy...Mother...of...God..." said Janna.

There seemed to be a bar between Gerta's eyes. And things had colors around them that hadn't been there before. Mousebones had a violet halo around his feathers. Janna was green and gold as summer.

The ground stank of reindeer blood—of her blood—and dark brown colors swirled up from the blood, like thin veins of smoke.

Gerta lifted her hooves to get away from the brown smoke and tried to shy away, except that it was everywhere around her.

"Easy," said Janna, and laughed in disbelief. "Easy, Gerta! Gerta?"

Gerta had to think what to do. A reindeer would have tilted her ears. Humans had stupid ears.

She nodded clumsily instead. It felt uncomfortable. Her antlers were a fan of swords, but her neck was a pillar to hold them up.

Mousebones landed on her antlers. "Awk! Awk!" He weighed nothing.

There was a clear place to the side. She gathered herself and jumped and halfway through she thought *wait, how do I—?* but then she landed and it hadn't been hard at all.

"Easy," whispered Janna, her voice lower. She caught Gerta around the neck, her hands full of the reindeer harness. "Can I— Lord! Is this okay?"

Gerta wanted to laugh. What came out was a soft wheezing sound. *Was* it okay? She didn't know.

She nodded again, ears flicking to catch the sounds of the approaching men.

Janna worked as swiftly as cold-numbed fingers would move, letting the straps out. "I'm sorry," she said. "You're bigger than he was. A lot bigger. You're not just him again. This is the strangest thing that has ever happened or ever will happen." She laughed herself, with a slightly hysterical edge, and then snapped her teeth down over it.

Gerta stood still while the other girl draped the harness over her shoulders. It didn't hurt. It felt normal.

Janna lifted the halter that was supposed to fit over a reindeer's ears. She looked at it, looked at Gerta, shook her head, and threw it into her pack. "Come on," she whispered. "Let's get out of here."

They moved through the forest as silently as they could, which wasn't very. Gerta's every step clacked as loudly as the old reindeer's had. Janna was still trying to fasten the wood-pigeon cage to the harness.

"Incidentally, they're about to find you," said Mousebones. Gerta flicked her ears, but there was no way to relay this to Janna. She walked forward, faster and faster, until Janna was jogging beside her.

The shouts behind them had a different note suddenly.

An arrow struck a tree with a crisp *zzzip!* sound.

Gerta, human, would have panicked. Gerta, reindeer, knew that she had to run, that running was the only way, but the human bit of her mind fought—*I can't run, if I run I'll leave Janna, what do I do?*

She dipped her muzzle under Janna's arm and pushed upward, her eyes white and rolling in her head. Another arrow struck nearby.

Janna flung her arms around Gerta's neck and put a leg over her back. She was heavy but the great reindeer heart in Gerta's chest beat and the muscles in her hindquarters pushed and then it was easy, ridiculously easy, and she lowered her head and ran, as fast as her legs would carry her.

Chapter Twenty-Five

She ran a long way, and she ran like a reindeer. The bushes parted in front of her and her legs knew where to strike to carry her forward and the important thing was to follow Mousebones and not to let her slow, stupid human mind get in the way of running.

The cries of the approaching bandits faded behind them, and the sound of arrows became the distant whine of mosquitoes, and then stopped entirely.

The raven led her out along the edge of the woods. It was easier in the open. There were no branches to tangle with her antlers. The air was cold and clear and swept the dark brown smell of blood away behind them.

When she could no longer run, she walked, and Janna slipped off her back and walked too.

"Are you all right?" she asked, and Gerta had to remember to nod her head up and down, like a sandpiper bobbing in the surf
but I've never seen a sandpiper
at the stony edge of the sea.

They walked for a little time, and then Gerta felt an urge to run again. She trotted a few steps, paused, looked back at Janna.

"You want me to ride?" asked Janna dubiously.

nod, nod, humans nod, crude gestures, nothing like the elegant flick of ears, a wolf could see a nod from a mile away

"Are you sure? I mean, when we're running away, that's one thing…"

you are so slow humans are slow up on their hind legs like birds

131

Mousebones laughed. "Careful," he said. "Careful, Gerta. That's the reindeer talking."

She tried to listen. *Gerta. Yes.* She took a deep breath and tried to remember that she was Gerta, a human girl, wearing a reindeer skin like a coat.

It did not feel like a coat. She felt like ink slowly dissolving in a cup of water, each swirl distinct but slowly, slowly running together.

I am not a reindeer, I am a girl, I am looking for my friend Kay, but I must walk the reindeer road to reach him.

"Better," said Mousebones. "Better."

Janna looked up at him. "I wish I knew what you were saying," she said.

"Awk!"

She has to ride, thought Gerta, *or else it will take years to get where we are going.*

And then, very faintly, like an echo without a sound to start it, *where* are *we going?*

She tucked her muzzle under Janna's elbow and flipped it up, impatient.

"Fine!" said Janna. "I get the point!"

"Awk! Awk!"

"This would be more comfortable if I had a saddle," said Janna. "But—ah—yeah, that might be crossing a line. Let me try to do something with cloaks."

She folded them and tucked them under the harness. It made no difference to Gerta either way.

Janna's weight on her back was welcome. It seemed to settle her more solidly against her bones. She began to trot and Janna leaned forward and fisted her hands in the shaggy hair at Gerta's withers.

They went on like that for many hours, walk and trot, walk and trot, until the light began to fail. As evening came on, Janna made as if to slip off, but Gerta shook her antlers and so they continued into the night.

The strange light that had settled on Gerta's vision helped. It was not that it was not dark, but the darkness itself was shot with bright threads.

The road that they were on ran north, a weave of blue and white. It was easy to follow. Even a reindeer with a human soul could not have missed it.

Mousebones had settled in to roost atop the cage of wood-pigeons. Janna rode with her chin tucked down and her cloak pulled up, her hands in her armpits to warm them.

It seemed to Gerta that some of the road-threads were plaiting themselves together oddly. The moon was rising, haloed by frost. Underneath it, the threads wove together, until Gerta was running on a long white braid of light.

And she was running. She had been running for some time, but it felt strangely effortless, as if the road was pulling her along it. She began to feel that she could have locked her legs, even lain down in the middle of the road, and the trees would still go rushing past her at a gallop.

Janna was lying almost flat against Gerta's back. She could feel the bandit girl's ribs rise and fall against her shoulders.

"What's happening?" said Janna.

Even if she had known, she could not have answered.

It should have been frightening, but it was not. It felt familiar. Surely someone had told Gerta stories of a road like this...somewhere...long ago?

She could almost hear her grandmother talking, but she could not make out the words.

It smelled like snow. It smelled like other reindeer.

If other reindeer had come this way, then it was safe.

The braid of light veered away from the human road. Gerta left that road without question. The strike of her hooves against the ground was oddly muffled, as if the glowing threads were taking her weight.

Janna made a small noise; half alarm, half resignation. Gerta felt the girl's fingers tightening in her hair. Humans had such small fingers. Good for things like scratching itchy spots, but useless for running.

If Mousebones had been awake, he might have said her name, but he slept with his head under his wing. There was no one to keep her from sinking into the reindeer dream.

The smell of other reindeer had grown stronger. She could make out individuals now—calf and cow, bull and matriarch. The echoes of their clicking hooves rang in her ears.

When the first one touched her, shoulder to shoulder, she was neither surprised nor frightened. *Of course, of course, there they are, here we are, we are running…*

Sight was the last sense to waken, but when it did she turned her head and saw them: the sea of antlers, the white backs, the ones who walked the reindeer road.

She was part of a herd and the herd was around her. She was not alone. While she was with the herd, she would never be alone.

Parts of her that were born lonely, as all humans are born lonely, were suddenly gathered up and loved and made one with the herd.

There were few human souls who could have stood against that.

Surrounded by the ghosts of reindeer, Gerta lowered her head and ran on, through the glowing threads of light.

Chapter Twenty-Six

There was no time on the reindeer road. She could not have said if it was an hour or a day or a year. The human mind that carved the world up into hours and minutes was deeply buried, while the reindeer heart ran on and on.

"Gerta," said Janna from her back, "where are we? Where did these reindeer come from?"

The words meant nothing. The reindeer dream was too strong for a human name to call her back.

It was Mousebones who saved them. He woke at last and looked around. "Awk! A long way! Awk!"

"I don't know what you're saying," said Janna. "I wish I did! I'd feel less like I was talking to myself."

Mousebones shook his feathers. "We'll run off the edge of the world at this rate. Next time, put a bridle on her—human fledglings in reindeer skins can't keep themselves for long."

He hopped across her neck, down between her antlers, and pecked Gerta hard between the eyes.

"Whuff!" said Gerta, startled.

Mousebones pecked her again, and then grabbed one of her ears in his talons. He yanked.

Gerta turned her head toward the tugging.

"That's right," said the raven. "Come on."

Alternating pecks and tugs, he steered her out of the main flow of the reindeer road. Ghostly bodies streamed past, their antlers a forest overhead.

The glowing threads were thinner here. Sometimes they tied together into knots and led outward. As Gerta swung her head, she saw some of her herdmates splitting off from the road, down the knots.

Mousebones cawed a question across the herd. "Which one?" he cried. "Which is this one?"

"Sápmi," said one of the reindeer, who seemed a trifle more solid than the rest. A living reindeer on the road, perhaps, not one of the vast spirit tide. "And that one, and the next."

"A very long way," said Mousebones. "Aurk! Well, as good as any."

He began steering her toward a knot, but Gerta resisted.

"Awk?"

"Not...this...one..." she said. The words were hard. They were human words spoken in the reindeer tongue, and they fitted together strangely.

"No?"

There was a fine glowing thread that was slightly different from the others. She had been following it for some time without quite realizing it.

It was only when her hooves left it that she recognized it for what it was.

It was bound to a knot up ahead, and it felt like an old woman sitting in a bar, telling stories.

"That...one..." said Gerta, pulling the words from some deep well.

"Very well," said Mousebones. "Very well. I hope this doesn't break us out in some wretched snowfield with nothing to eat."

She ran on.

It was only a little way to the next knot, although what that meant in time or miles, she did not know. But she veered off the reindeer road and her hooves struck the knot and the threads unbraided themselves around her.

Between one stride and the next, the herd of reindeer faded away. She felt a last few ghosts go with her, shoulder on shoulder, and then they too were gone and she was back, alone, in the world of humans and ravens.

The loss of the herd fell on her like a blow. She had not known that she needed one until it was gone. Her bones and her sinews cried out against it, and she tried to swerve back on the reindeer road.

Mousebones pecked her hard between the eyes. "None of that!"

"I felt that," said Janna, sitting up. Gerta could feel the girl's weight shifting on her back. "What happened?"

"We went a little outside of the world," said Mousebones. "A shortcut, maybe. Like a tunnel carved by the dreams of reindeer." After a moment he added, "Dead reindeer, mostly. And not one of them there enough to eat. Awk!"

Janna looked at him and shook her head. "You're saying something," she said, "but I have no idea what it is. I wish I did."

"Awk," said Mousebones.

Gerta dropped her head. Listening to her friends talk at each other eased the ache in her chest a little. They were a small herd, and strangely shaped, but still better than being a reindeer alone.

Janna slid off Gerta's back and wrapped an arm over her withers. "Are you all right? We went...I don't know how far we went."

She glanced around. "We went all night, anyway. I didn't think people rode all night except in stories."

It was not yet dawn. The air was cold and grey and smelled of frost. The ground under Gerta's hooves was frozen hard.

Mousebones took to the air. He flew into the dimness, muttering about visibility.

"Come on," said Janna. "Let's walk. If you were a horse, you'd have to walk after all that running. I don't know if reindeer do that."

She pressed a hand on Gerta's neck, and Gerta took a few steps forward, then a few more. She could feel her muscles trembling.

"This is all quite ridiculous," Janna said. Gerta flicked an ear back toward her. "I couldn't tell anyone about it. *Oh, yes, this reindeer? This is actually a pretty little blond girl who turned up on my doorstep with a story about the Snow Queen.*" She snorted. "They'd think I was mad. Perhaps I am. Still, even if I'm mad, I can't do much but carry on. I suppose most people who are mad are still doing the next logical thing, aren't they? If you were in there, you'd see it all made perfect sense. Maybe not people like Old Nan, but that's because she's cruel, not because she's mad."

Her voice was a little muffled. Gerta realized after a moment that Janna's teeth were chattering. Gerta herself was all too warm. She leaned into Janna a little, trying to warm her, and the bandit girl laughed. "Careful! You'll knock me over."

Mousebones landed on her antlers with a harsh caw. "Close!" he said. "There's a village or something like it."

Janna looked up at him. "Found something?"

The raven muttered something about humans that thought they were the only species with anything worth saying. "Bear left, Gerta."

Gerta bore left.

The village that Mousebones had found was very small, and the buildings seemed to grow out of the ground in irregular domes. Gerta smelled peat and smoke. A little outside of town, there was a house that looked almost like the cabins and farmhouses Gerta had passed in human days, but it was up on tree trunks and stood over the rest of the houses like a hen towering over chicks.

There were threads glowing here, too, akin to the ones on the reindeer road. They drifted lazily around the mound houses, snaking between buildings.

One of the houses was wrapped tightly with the threads, and there was a woman standing in front of it.

"Well!" she said. "Took you long enough!"

"Were you waiting for us?" asked Janna.

"Does that surprise you?"

Janna laughed hoarsely. "Nothing would surprise me today. I may never be surprised again."

"Ah, well." The woman smiled, turning her eyes into a mass of wrinkles. She had broad cheekbones and a broader smile and everything else was so wrapped in knit blankets that there was no telling about the shape underneath. "You're young yet. Let us get your friend loose."

The woman walked around Gerta, trailing her hand over the reindeer body's long furry flanks. "Goodness. Went deep, didn't she?"

"She walked the reindeer road," said Mousebones. "Awk!"

"Dangerous thing for a human to walk," said the woman. "Even in a reindeer skin. Maybe especially in a reindeer skin."

"Lord!" said Janna. "Don't tell me you understand him too?"

"The raven? Sure. Ravens are easy, though they'll talk your ear off and they think they're God's gift to the world."

"Awk!"

"Hush."

She set her hands over the base of Gerta's antlers and spoke words, then, words that Gerta did not recognize, the same words three times over, and then recited the Lord's Prayer.

The two halves of Gerta's vision converged suddenly and the world was deeper and darker. The bright braids of light went away. The woman's blankets shown red and white and green, not just shades of brown and grey.

Gerta was on her knees in the snow, with the reindeer skin over her. It felt heavy and sticky and in her veins, the blood moved thin and hot.

"My heart is smaller," she whispered.

"Of course," said the woman. "Reindeer have greater hearts than humans. They have to, to give us as much as they do." She pulled the reindeer hide back, ignoring the stickiness, and helped Gerta to her feet.

"Are you a witch?" asked Janna.

139

"No," said the old woman, "I'm a Lutheran. But we'll make do. My name's Livli. Bring your friend inside."

Chapter Twenty-Seven

"Naked and bloody we come into the world, and sometimes we go out of it the same way." Livli draped a blanket over Gerta's shoulders. "But it's not a good way to spend the parts in between. I'll heat some water for you."

Gerta's clothes had gone somewhere, but that was probably for the best. Freed of the thick coat of reindeer hair, her skin felt raw and over-sensitive, as if she had a full-body sunburn. Even the touch of the blanket was nearly unbearable. She could practically feel each thread in the weave.

She was sitting on a wooden chest with a blanket thrown over it, which was nearly as bad. Where the edge of the lid pressed against the backs of her knees felt like a band of iron.

How did humans go around, feeling things on every inch of their skin all the time? How had *she* gone around, before?

I used to just ignore this, she thought wonderingly, rolling the edge of the blanket between her fingers. *I would hardly notice it at all. How did I do that?*

Janna, perhaps mistaking her expression, came and sat beside her. "It will be all right," she said, in a voice indicating that it damn well better be, or she'd know the reason why.

Gerta nodded. It was easier than trying to talk.

The bandit girl studied her for a moment, then reached out and took her hand, and Gerta no longer thought she could talk. Every whorl and ridge on Janna's fingertips seemed to stand out in sharp relief, and there was a long bar across the heel of her hand that might have been a scar.

Where their wrists lay together, she could feel Janna's pulse beating, stronger and slower than hers.

It was too much. She disentangled her hands and put her face in them to try and blot out a little of the world.

"You'll feel better in a bit," said Livli, poking up the fire in the belly of the stove.

"Will I?" Gerta asked.

"I haven't the faintest idea," said Livli. She smiled. "Sounded comforting, though, and that's worth something. I've never met anyone who's borrowed a reindeer skin before. You'll have to explain how it happened to me."

Gerta spread her fingers so that she could look out at Janna. Janna opened her mouth, closed it, and looked helplessly back at Gerta.

In the end it was Mousebones who explained. The raven hopped into the curved rafters, which were hung with cords full of dried meat.

From his perch above, he called down the story. It was slightly more bird-centric than Gerta remembered, but seemed mostly true, and after a time she stopped listening.

She was almost falling asleep, despite the painful sensitivity of her skin, when Mousebones said "Awk! What was her human name, Gerta?"

Gerta licked her lips. They were dry and each crack was a canyon and lord, even her tongue against her teeth was a sensation that had to be recognized and catalogued and put away somewhere in her mind. "Who?" she asked.

"The old woman with the sausages."

"Gran..." said Gerta. "Gran...Aischa. Yes."

Livli cackled. "I might have known! Well, I did know you were coming, truth be told, but I wasn't sure who sent you to me."

"How did you know?" asked Janna. She sounded as tired as Gerta felt, but still sharp enough to question.

"A wood beetle told me, and an owl, and the track of snow geese against the sky. I knew something was coming."

Janna raised an eyebrow. "A wood beetle? Really?"

Livli grinned. She had excellent teeth. "The wood beetle might have been a coincidence. I am nearly certain about the owl, though." She poured hot water from a kettle into a cup and threw herbs in it. The scent of tea filled the dark house. "I talk to birds," she said, by way of explanation. "That's all I can do, but it's stood me in good stead so far."

Gran Aischa said to find Livli. This is Livli. Coincidence? No, surely not. I must have been following some thread as a reindeer, looking…

There was something that Gerta was supposed to tell the Sámi woman, but she could not quite remember.

There were three old women rattling together in her head— Livli and Old Nan and Gran Aischa. *The good one and the evil one and the one in the middle, all of them tied together with stories of the Snow Queen…*

A proper fairy tale arrangement. Gran Aischa would be delighted.

Just like that, she remembered what she was supposed to tell Livli. "Gran Aischa told me to tell you…to tell you…"

"Drink first." Livli pressed a cup of tea into Gerta's hands, and the heat was good. It almost burned, but if she was focusing on the heat of the cup, she was not feeling the blanket or the chest beneath her, or the way that Janna's hip touched hers as they sat together on the chest.

She took a drink, and it burned hot and fragrant down her throat and made her gasp.

In a proper fairy tale, there would be magical herbs in it, but Gerta thought that it was only tea—and tea was more than enough. She had been drinking tea when she was barely old enough to hold a mug. The cup was carved from a wooden burl and the handle was made of bone, but it was still familiar. *Yes. This I understand.*

The world settled a little more comfortably around her. She was a girl who had briefly worn a reindeer skin, not a reindeer squashed into the awkward body of a human.

"She said my story was written on the hides of herring."

Livli threw back her head and laughed. "Oh my! Yes, it is, isn't it?"

"What does it mean?" Gerta asked.

"Oh, well." The Sámi woman leaned back, testing the hot water again. "Bit of a joke between Aisha and I. She was always telling stories, and if I told her one back, she'd pick it up and embroider it all out of reason. I got tired of it after awhile, and told her that if she wanted to tell me a fish story again, she'd best send it written on the hides of herring."

She shook her head. "And here you are, and a ridiculous story the raven's told me. And yet I believe every word. Strange, isn't it?"

Gerta slept most of the day under a reindeer hide that was not raw and bloody. It was soft and warm and she had half-expected to find it terrifying, but it was not. The owner had died and surely its ghost moved somewhere on the reindeer road. The skin wanted to be useful, that was all.

Sleeping with the reindeer hide wrapped around her, with Janna back-to-back against her, was a little like being in a herd again.

As close, perhaps, as a human could hope to be.

Chapter Twenty-Eight

She woke alone, except for the cooing of the doves still in their cage. *We will have to do something about them*, she thought groggily, *we cannot go to the end of the world with doves. If Livli can talk to birds, perhaps she'll be able to explain to them what's going on.*

And then slightly more awake, she thought, *Are we going to the end of the world, then?*

Near enough, I suppose. And who is we? *Mousebones and I and... is Janna coming, as well?*

The thought caught oddly in her throat. She shouldn't care, of course—she'd known Janna for what, three days? Four? And she hadn't even been human for one of those days, and Janna had been one of her captors...

Well, no. That's not fair. She didn't capture me. And she got me free as soon as she could, and she left her father behind in order to do it... not that she seemed to care too much about it...

The doves cooed and rattled their cage again.

I suppose that's what I am. A great big human dove that fluttered in and Janna put me in a cage until she could figure out what to do with me.

The thought should have been demeaning, but she found it oddly cheering. After weeks on her own, Gerta was prepared to be grateful to find anyone at all who was on her side.

The door opened and Janna herself came in, stamping her feet. "You're awake," she said. "Do you know where we are?"

"Sápmi, I think?" said Gerta, sitting up.

"Sápmi," agreed Janna. "Did Mousebones tell you, then? Livli, the old woman, she's Sámi."

"Okay?" Gerta knew nothing at all about the Sámi, except that they lived in the north and drove reindeer and her grandmother had said once that they were the most ruthlessly taxed people in all the world.

"I had no idea we'd come so far," said Janna. "I've always wanted to come here. Though I might have come in summer instead. It's cold out there." She blew on her hands.

"Are you all right?" asked Gerta.

"Oh, sure. Doing chores, that's all. Half the village is off somewhere—they camp in hide tents in this cold! Can you imagine?—and Livli's got no grandsons to do the heavy work. I get the impression that her people'll do anything she asks, but she doesn't like to need to ask. So I've been swinging an ice axe all afternoon to try to pay for the supplies we're going to be taking."

Gerta ran her fingers through her hair and scrambled into the clothes that Livli had left her. They were shapeless and worn and two sizes too long, but her own clothes were gone somewhere—part of the reindeer hide now or something. She was gladder to hear the *we* part than she liked to admit.

Livli herself came in, carrying an armload of something that looked like bark, but which were actually dried fish. She began poking up the fire and dropping the fish into the stewpot. "Are you human this morning, my dear, or reindeer?"

"Human, I think," said Gerta. "Mostly, anyway." Her skin no longer felt as raw as a newborn's. She stroked her fingers over the reindeer hide she'd slept on. *Herd herd herd* chimed in her bones, the faintest of echoes, like hoofbeats far away in the fog.

Livli nodded. "I should think that the longer you spend out of the skin, the more human you'll feel. And the other way around.

Stay in it too long, and you likely won't want to come out again. At least, that's what the swans tell me, and they know more about changing skins than most birds."

"Will I have to do it again?" asked Gerta. *Do I want to? It didn't feel bad...just different...*

"If you're determined to find your friend, then yes," said Livli. "The Snow Queen's land is north of here. North and east and north again. If you can reach it in any fashion at all, it will be by the reindeer road."

Janna's frown deepened. She looked as if she were about to say something, but there was a tap on the door, and she went to open it.

Mousebones hopped inside, looking disgruntled. "Awk! Leave a raven out in the cold, why don't you?"

"Should have known you'd show up when the food was cooking," said Livli, amused. She tossed him a dried fish and he pounced on it.

"I suppose we'll take the reindeer road again, then," said Gerta. "If it's the only way to find Kay."

The name Kay sounded odd on her lips. For a moment he seemed like a character out of a childhood story, like the Snow Queen herself.

Don't be silly. It's Kay, who kissed me behind the stove, and who played games with me when it was snowing and who has bright blue eyes and who is my best friend...

Her mind veered off at that point, and Janna interrupted her thoughts by asking, "What if I wear the skin instead?"

"Can't," said Livli. "Oh, I'm sure you'd try, don't get me wrong. But you're too set in your own skin. You're a healthy young animal and you know it. And people who really live in their own flesh and know it and love it make lousy shapechangers."

"I...well. But Gerta doesn't?"

Livli shook her head. "Some people don't. Their bodies carry them around, but they don't live in them quite the same way."

She leaned over and patted Gerta's hand. "Don't look so stricken, dear. It's not a personal failing. And I think there may be something else at work here, too. You're outside your own skin even farther than you ought to be. Have you had a long illness recently?"

Gerta started to deny it, and then remembered the witch and her long waking dream. "...uh," she said, and explained, as best she could, what it had been like to wake up seven months older, in a body that no longer fit around her the way that it should have.

"Ah!" Livli looked briefly pleased, and then indignant. "How dreadful. Something will have to be done. We are all of us lonely, but we don't go kidnapping children and keeping them wrapped under spells so they don't leave. That's mother-love twisted around and gone sour."

She leaned back. "Well, it'll get sorted. But that's not quite it either. You've got something, Gerta. Or...not got it?"

"No magic," said Mousebones from the rafters. "Unmagic until it's almost something in itself. *I* said she was like a branch covered in frost."

"Yes..." said Livli slowly. "Yes, I can see that. You're like an empty pot that someone poured magic into and poured out again."

Gerta did not much like being called an empty pot. Livli laughed at her expression. "Peace, child, it's not a failing on your part. It's not that you're weak-willed or anything like that."

"But I am weak-willed," said Gerta glumly. "If I wasn't, the witch would never have caught me."

Livli shook her head. "You may be or not be, but it's no bearing on the matter. Being an empty vessel, magic will always take you very hard, I think, and leave something of itself behind for a time, like dregs at the bottom. But at the same time, it can't really get at the core of you. You can be filled up and emptied out, but the pot does not become its contents. Does that make sense?"

"A little, I suppose," said Gerta. It sounded rather dreadful when put like that. Was she going to spend her life wandering around being filled up with other people's enchantments?

"Well, then." Livli sat back. "The hide is safest on you. You will change easily, but I do not think you will get completely lost in it."

Janna still looked rebellious. "But—"

"If nothing else," said Livli, "it was a gift to her, and gifts given freely are a bit less likely to turn bad on you. It's a thin bit of luck, but there you are."

"I'll take all the luck I can get," said Gerta determinedly. She was the one who had to find Kay. This was her journey, after all. And if she was going to stop being weak-willed, then she should start now. "Janna, it's all right. You got me away from…ah…the bandits…"

Janna's lips quirked as Gerta stumbled over this phrase. "Well," she said. "More or less, yes." She slipped her arm through Gerta's.

Gerta was prepared to feel annoyed by this and was a bit surprised to find that she didn't. Janna's hands were warm and her arm was solid. The part of her that was still a reindeer wanted to lean against the bandit girl, shoulder to shoulder and hip to hip: *herd, herd, herd.*

This was a strange set of thoughts to be running under the human ones. Gerta shook her head and would have flicked her ears if she had ears worth flicking.

Livli was looking at her. Gerta had a feeling that the old woman knew what she was thinking, and felt vaguely embarrassed. She lifted her chin defiantly.

"I'll wear the hide," she said.

"Is there some other way?" asked Janna. "Some way that you can teach me?"

"Teach you what?" asked Livli. "Don't think that I have answers!"

The stove popped and cracked. Janna made a small sound of frustration, rather like the stove.

Livli reached out and tapped the bandit girl's knee. "I am not trying to be unkind here. This is not a Sámi thing. We don't take our skins off any more often than anybody else. Less often than some, if you believe all the stories of wolf-skin walkers from the south. There are stories of *noaidi* from long ago turning into birds, to lure flocks north to Sápmi, but those are only stories. I'm in the dark nearly as much as you."

"But you seem to know all about it!" said Gerta, surprised.

Livli laughed. "What I know, I know from talking to ravens and swans. Birds are terrible gossips. They know as much about shapechanging as anyone, although swans won't tell you everything they know, and ravens think they know everything worth knowing already. You've not got a swan with you, so it's up to your raven."

"Awk," said Mousebones. "And I *do* know everything worth knowing. Almost." He snapped off a flaky brown chunk of fish and swallowed it down.

"At any rate," said Livli, sitting back, "the swans tell me that shapechanging is easier when your own shape does not quite fit. The door inside your skin is a little way open—or at least, I think that is the human equivalent of what they are saying. Swans don't speak of doors, and they have very sharp minds." She rubbed her forehead, as if to banish an old headache. "So children when their bodies change to adults, and old women when they are becoming crones…and girls pregnant for the first time, though that often ends badly for all involved."

Gerta dropped her eyes, faintly embarrassed. "No chance of that," she murmured.

Janna gave her an amused, unreadable glance out of the corner of her eye.

"You'll need a sled," said Livli, passing over the awkwardness. "It will be much easier than riding. Gerta can pull it, but Janna, you'll have to take her out every night. Both the harness and the hide."

Janna nodded. "How do I do it?"

"I imagine you'll have to cut her out," said Livli. "Not a deep cut. Tickle her throat with a knife, eh?"

Janna winced. She reached across the space between them and gripped Gerta's hand tightly. Gerta squeezed back, wondering who needed more comfort.

Being cut out of the skin does not sound pleasant at all.

"It won't be quite so bad," said Livli. "The skin remembers the knife that cut it. Usually."

"*You* didn't use a knife," said Janna.

"Get to be my age, girl, and your tongue will be as sharp as one. Then you can try cutting someone out of a skin with words alone. Until then, it's the blade or nothing."

Janna exhaled slowly.

"That's the other reason it has to be Gerta in the skin," said Livli. "Of the two of you, who do you think could cut the other's throat, and do it again and again, for however many days it takes you to reach the farthest north?"

Janna's fingers closed convulsively tight. Gerta laid her free hand on the other girl's shoulder, not sure what to say or if there was anything *to* say.

We are so far beyond what is normal here, there are no words. My grandmother never told me any stories about this. Kay and I…

She looked down at Janna's dark fingers laced with her own pale ones. She could not think of anything that she and Kay had ever done that had mattered half so much or had been even half so strange.

"You must not let her sleep as a reindeer," said Livli. "Not if you can avoid it. I don't know this for certain, the birds never told me, but my gut says she'll go so deep that getting her out again will be a job for saints, not women. I don't say that she *can't* come back—there are stories of people who have come back from years in wolf skin, but they aren't right afterwards, not by a long stretch."

"So I cut her throat at night, or I—*we* lose her completely?" asked Janna. She gave a hoarse bark of laughter. "When you fetched up on the doorstep, Gerta, if I'd realized what this would be like…"

"You don't have to come," said Gerta. It hurt her to say it, more than it should have. "I'm sure Mousebones can...I'm sure there's another way."

"No," said Janna. She released Gerta's hand and pinched the bridge of her nose between her fingers. "No, I'll do it. You always want someone you trust to hold the knife, hey?"

Do I trust you? thought Gerta. *I barely know you and you frightened me and then you kissed me, and truth be told, that frightened me even more.*

Livli smirked. "I bet it's not the first throat you've cut, girl," she said.

Janna gave her a wry look. "No," she said, "but it's never been anyone I *liked.*"

This was a reminder that Gerta hadn't really wanted, even as Livli laughed.

Well. Still, it is probably better to take someone who can cut throats along. Who knows what it will take to get Kay away from the Snow Queen?

"Tomorrow, then," said Livli, and both girls nodded.

Chapter Twenty-Nine

In her dreams that night, Gerta saw Marten die. She saw it in far greater detail than she had seen it in reality, every drop of blood the size of an apple, striking the snow and staining it red. The bolt grew to the size of a tree trunk and she watched him twist and fall, over and over, until she woke up gasping.

Janna's back was against hers. Her breathing was slow and even. *Yes. I'm awake. I'm alive. It's not happening. It isn't real.*

Except that it was real, and the man was dead.

She curled her fingers in the reindeer hide.

She wasn't mourning for him. She hadn't known him, and what she knew she didn't like. He'd done violence to her and to Janna both.

No, it's more…it was just…there. In front of me.

I've never seen anyone die before.

Her father had died when Gerta was very small, but she did not remember it. She sighed and settled herself more solidly against Janna's back. The other girl mumbled something, gave half a snore, and subsided.

When Gerta fell asleep again, she dreamed of plants.

There were bands of trees a long way off, but this part of Sápmi was low grass and meadow. The plants slept beneath the snow, or had died outright and were only dreaming seeds.

The plants knew the teeth of reindeer, and the reindeer knew the taste of plants. Gerta sank into a dream that ran like the reindeer road, free of thought, the living and the dead going on together, on and on forever.

Livli brought out a reindeer sled the next morning; or rather, had two Sámi men drag it out from storage. The two men laughed and joked, flirted with Janna in the few words that were common between them, and then took themselves away as soon as Livli shooed them off.

"They're good lads," she said fondly. "But if they sit and watch girls turning into reindeer, they'll ask too many questions."

"Won't they wonder where the sled has gone?"

"Certainly. I'll tell them I traded it to a smashing young man in return for a night of passion. It'll do my reputation no end of good."

Gerta raised both eyebrows. "Will they believe you?"

"Probably not, but they won't dare ask any questions for fear of getting more details."

Livli herself took down the reindeer hide.

"I've cleaned it," she said, "and stretched it a little. It's all I dare do. The swans do something to their feather cloaks that keeps them supple, but they won't tell an outsider how they do it." She shook out the hide, like a cloak. The inside was faintly pink. "Scrub it down with handfuls of snow. It won't last forever, but the cold will keep it from rotting out while you need it. When it's done, give it to *Jábmiidáhkká.*"

Gerta felt, by this point, that it was better to admit ignorance. The world had proved all too full of things that she didn't know that could hurt her. "I'm sorry," she said, "I don't know what that means."

Mousebones, perched on the top of the house, cawed once. "The Mother of the Dead," he said.

"What the raven said. Bury it," Livli said. "Under scree or under earth."

"I'm sorry," said Gerta, feeling that she had failed somehow. "I didn't know—"

Livli patted her arm. "No reason you should, I suppose. You've got your own gods to deal with. But reindeer belong to our gods, and our gods belong to them."

"I thought you were Lutheran," said Janna.

"I am. Doesn't mean I'm stupid, girl. Luther lived a long ways away. *Jábmiidáhkká* lives under my feet. And I've never heard that Luther had much to do with reindeer, which was clearly a failing in an otherwise upright man."

She held out the hide. "Enough. It'll last as long as you need it. Don't expect to be walking the road when you're old, unless you find another way."

Gerta nodded and took the hide.

It went on more easily this time, or perhaps she did not fear it— *or perhaps I am simply not panicked and ready to run from bandits*—

And then she was a reindeer.

She tested it this time, delicately. Her legs were so long, and they clacked with every step, a signal to others in the herd *here I am here I am here.*

When she drew breath, her lungs filled more deeply than a human's lungs could, and the cold air was sharp and wonderful and made her feel alive.

She tried to bounce on her hooves, but it came out as a buck instead. She walked, one step at a time, and then she ran.

The reindeer body was swift and strong and it understood running. Mousebones flew alongside her, laughing his cawing raven laugh.

At last, she settled, and trotted demurely back to Livli and Janna. Both of them were grinning.

"That looked like fun," said Janna.

Gerta remembered how to nod and did so, vigorously.

"Ah, that's a good use of a skin," said Livli. "Seals and reindeer have the best of it, I think."

"Ravens can fly," said Mousebones, sounding affronted.

"Swans can fly, too," said Livli. "But they never seem to be enjoying it much. Come on, Gerta, let's get this harness on you and see if you can pull a sled."

The sled was ridiculously easy to pull. Gerta stood while Livli fussed over straps and belts, muttering to herself. "Your skin comes from a *heargi*—one of the draft males—and you're about the same size."

"He was smaller," said Janna, "but it might just have been that he was thin."

Livli nodded. "They get thinner as they get old. The truly ancient ones, you can practically see the wind through their bones. Lower your head, Gerta, I'm putting a bridle on you."

"Err," said Janna. "Is that...uh..."

"If she goes deep into the dream, you'll want a way to catch her," said Livli practically.

Tell them I don't mind, said Gerta to Mousebones.

He told them. Livli nodded.

Janna sighed. "I wish I could talk to ravens."

The bridle didn't hurt. There was no bit like a horse would have. The strap behind her ears felt like her hair had been newly braided, and was still tight against her scalp.

"It's the principle," said Janna. "You start putting tack on people..." She shook her head.

"We've been putting tack on four-legged people for thousands of years," said Livli.

"People who can talk."

"Plenty of four-legged people can talk. Not everybody listens well. Never got the trick of it, myself, but beasts are quieter than birds."

Janna threw her hands in the air. "Fine, fine! I will keep my objections to myself." Mousebones snickered.

Livli hitched Gerta-as-reindeer up to the sled, and then undid it all and made Janna do it again while she watched. Once she was satisfied, she slapped Gerta's flank and said, "Pull and see how that works."

Gerta pulled.

It was easy. It was ridiculously easy. Janna climbed onto the sled and that was a little heavier, but the reindeer body knew how to pull on some level deeper than thought. It was what reindeer *did*. Gerta threw her shoulders into it and her haunches and the sled slid over the snow-slick ground and it was all so *easy*.

She felt powerful.

It was such an unexpected sensation that she would have laughed, if reindeer could laugh above a gentle wheezing. It had not occurred to her before that she was weak. She had been a perfectly average young human, if a bit short. But she had never before felt *strong*.

I am strong, she said to Mousebones, astonished.

"Awk! Very strong! And I am clever," said the raven, laughing for both of them. "We ought to be unstoppable now."

Livli snorted. "The Snow Queen will be stronger than either of you," she said. "Nothing is stronger than winter. I don't know about clever, though."

Mousebones looked smug. Gerta snorted and stamped her hoof.

"Well," said Livli. "That's sorted. Now for the last bit. Janna."

"Must we?" asked Janna, sounding lost and a little forlorn.

Livli snorted. "Better to practice it now. Do you want to try for the first time tomorrow night, with no one to help you if aught goes wrong?"

Janna swallowed. She stepped up to Gerta's head and caught the bridle under the chin.

Gerta braced her hooves. *I will not run. I will not.*

It was surprisingly easy not to run. Janna was the herd, and you did not run from the herd.

Janna leaned forward and rested her forehead against Gerta's, between the eyes.

"What are you waiting for?" asked Livli. "A magic knife?"

"If you have one, yes!"

The old woman snorted. "Knives aren't magic, girl. All they are is sharp. Cut or don't, but don't dither over it. It only makes it worse for both of you."

Janna let out a single dry sob and set the point of her knife against Gerta's throat.

She did not hesitate for long.

In the end, it hurt differently than Gerta expected.

The blade was very sharp. There was hardly any pain, only a hot sting—but either Janna was slow or the cut was far longer than she expected, and Gerta felt the dreadful queasy feeling of cold metal being dragged through her flesh.

It lasted three heartbeats, no more.

Then, as if the point of the knife were the axis of the world, everything flipped over. It was not her skin being cut any more, it was the reindeer hide flapping open and she was inside it.

She staggered. Janna flung the knife aside and threw her arms around Gerta's shoulders.

"I'm sorry," she said thickly. Gerta thought that the bandit girl was crying. "I'm so sorry."

"It's all right," said Gerta, still a little dazed from being a reindeer. She had not sunk so deeply into the dream that time, and her skin was only a little tender. The harness flapped loose and ridiculous around her shoulders. She would pull it off in a moment, but she didn't want to push Janna away. "It's all right. It only hurts a little."

Janna took a shuddering breath and stepped back. She was paler than Gerta had thought she could be. "You're bleeding."

Gerta put a hand to her neck. There was a narrow line of heat, more sore than painful. "Am I?"

"Cut any deeper than the skin, and she'll bleed plenty," said Livli. "Cut long and shallow. You didn't do badly, though."

Gerta shook off the harness and squared her shoulders. "Do you think you can do that again?"

Janna met her eyes, only for a moment, then had to look away. "If I must," she said, and picked up the fallen knife.

Chapter Thirty

They set out early the next day.

The nights were long, this far north, and would get no shorter until the year turned. So Gerta took the reindeer shape when it was still dark and Janna hitched her to the sled and Mousebones grumbled about the hour.

"The blessing of the saints upon you," said Livli. "If you can bring down the Snow Queen, so much the better. That's an old spirit, and not a kind one. But if all you can do is get your friend away, that's not a failure, either."

"Thank you," said Janna. "I know I—we—appreciate it. Without you, I don't know how…"

Livli snorted. "Don't worry about it. Aischa sent you to me, and it's the least I can do to send you on. Both of you. I doubt you'll come free of Gerta's story easily."

Janna gave a short, pained laugh and climbed onto the sled.

"I've packed you food," said Livli. "Fish, not reindeer. I thought perhaps you wouldn't want to eat that at the moment." She slapped Gerta's flank. "Go well."

When they were out of sight of Livli's home, Janna said "I left her money. A sled's worth a lot around here, even an old one like this. I didn't want to make a big deal out of it, but it matters." Gerta nodded her head up and down. There was no paying for the aid they had gotten, but for the sled, one could at least give a good price.

Gerta found the reindeer road easily. The threads of light were strong here, pounded down by a thousand hooves.

"And here we are again," muttered Janna, as they swung onto the road. "Ah, it's worse down low like this." She pulled her cloak up over her head. Mousebones perched at the front of the sled and snickered.

After that, it was only running.

There were living reindeer on the road as well as ghosts, which startled Gerta a little, and yet they seemed as glad to see her as any of the others. She ran alongside a young male, barely more than a calf, for a long way, their hooves striking in unison, and it was good.

They parted to allow the sled to pass, as if it were perfectly normal. Perhaps it was. The generosity of the reindeer to a human in their midst—and a human in their skin—should not have surprised her, and yet it did.

She did not sink as deeply into the reindeer dream this time. The short day passed swiftly, but Mousebones was there to call her back each time.

Perhaps you can get used to anything, thought Gerta.

Perhaps it would be too easy to get used to this.

It had been dark for several hours, and Mousebones said "Pull off, Gerta, or I'll fall asleep. Ravens weren't meant to gallivant around in the dark."

The landscape, when they left the reindeer road, was much like the one they had left in Sápmi—fields of snow-covered scree and distant trees. Gerta was still looking around her, wondering vaguely if there was somewhere to graze, when Janna came up and caught her beneath the chin.

"I'm sorry," she said, and cut.

The skin fell away around the point of the knife. Gerta emerged, shaking off the hide, and Janna caught her.

"I hate this," said the bandit girl, to no one in particular.

"Was it easier that time?" asked Gerta.

"Yes," said Janna. "That's what I hate."

Her voice was matter-of-fact, and her hand on the knife had been steady. But Gerta looked up into her eyes and the naked anguish there was more than she could stand.

With barely any more thought than to stop that hurt, Gerta stepped forward and kissed her.

Janna made a tiny noise of surprise and then her arms came down around Gerta's shoulders. One hand slid up the back of her neck.

Gerta thought for an instant that wearing the reindeer hide had left her skin raw again. Then she thought that perhaps she would have felt every fingertip on her skin burn like a brand anyway, and then Janna's mouth opened over hers and she stopped thinking entirely.

She regained a little bit of sense when Janna sheathed the knife. *Oh, right, of course, has she been holding it all this time...?*

Then Janna slid her free hand up over Gerta's breast, and no one had ever touched her like that, and good Lord, why not—*no, no, it's probably good, I might die, but that's okay, I'd rather die than stop this—*

They had to stop eventually. It was sooner than Gerta would have liked, but the wind was howling and she was wearing nothing but a few leather straps and some very cold buckles.

"You'll freeze," said Janna hoarsely, pulling off her cloak and draping it over Gerta. "I—oh God! I can't."

"Can't what?" asked Gerta.

"Can't tumble you right here and be damned." Janna barked a laugh, short and sharp as a jay calling. "I want to. I can't."

"Can't?" said Gerta. (Did she want to be tumbled? What would that involve, exactly? It seemed like a bad time to ask.)

Janna reached out and dragged her fingertips over Gerta's cheekbone, down the side of her neck. "I can't," she said. "I shouldn't. I'm strapping you up in harnesses in the morning and cutting your throat at night. The inside of my head is getting twisted up enough already. I'll end up with a terrible passion for reindeer or something even worse."

Gerta had to laugh at that. "Are you sure?"

"No. Not remotely." Janna's fingers stroked over Gerta's collarbone, down the line of her breast—Gerta held her breath—and then she sighed deeply and laid her palm flat over Gerta's heart. "I am the world's greatest fool," she said, and took her hand away.

"Humans," said Mousebones, with deep disgust. "You can't even figure out how to mate properly." He stalked away into the snow with as much dignity as a walking raven could manage.

Gerta swallowed hard. She'd offered…something…and been rejected.

She wasn't even entirely sure *what* she'd offered, only that it hadn't been accepted.

Janna searched her face. "After," said the bandit girl, taking her hand. "After all this is over, after you're done being a reindeer—"

She folded her fingers around Gerta's and kissed each knuckle. Gerta watched her do it. The wind was freezing cold, but her skin felt burning hot.

They put up the tent together. There is hardly anything romantic about putting up tents, but every time their hands touched, Gerta felt it down to her bones.

It was a clear night and there were ten thousand stars. But it was also burning cold, and they stayed outside the tent only long enough to make hot tea and eat. Livli had given them dried fish jerky, which was…edible, anyway.

"I've had better," muttered Janna.

"It's salty," said Gerta, tearing at hers with her teeth. "I really want salt right now. Salt is amazing."

"Reindeer do love salt," said Janna. "I suppose it's not impossible that stuck with you…"

Gerta paused, alarmed, but only a moment.

"I suppose it'll wear off eventually," she said. "Once I'm not wearing the skin every day."

When they had finished—or when their jaws were too tired to chew off any more fish—Janna banked the fire and they crawled inside the tent.

It was too dark to see each other. There were only sounds and rustling and Mousebones making irritable noises. And yet Gerta was incredibly aware of where Janna was, of the sound of her breathing, and her stomach clenched even though she knew that nothing was going to happen that night.

And what do I want to happen, after all?

"Would you really end up with a terrible passion for reindeer?" asked Gerta, when she could not stand the charged silence any longer.

In the darkness inside the tent, Janna snorted. "Probably not that, no. But the cutting…there are some things you shouldn't do to your lovers." She coughed and added something under her breath that Gerta didn't quite catch.

"I don't mind," said Gerta. "Truly."

Janna sighed. "*I* mind," she said. "And my sanity is not quite so solid that I can keep putting a knife against your throat, night after night, and not bleed for it."

Gerta reached out and found Janna's hand, and squeezed.

"All right," she said, and Janna squeezed back.

They said nothing for a little while, and Janna's breathing evened out, and the wind muttered around the outside of the tent.

"Afterward, though?" said Gerta, finally. Her voice was very small, in case Janna was asleep.

The bandit girl rolled over, so that her face was against Gerta's shoulder.

"After," said Janna. "And I hope your friend is worth it."

Chapter Thirty-One

In the morning, when the tent was broken down and the fire stamped out, Janna handed her the reindeer hide. But she pressed a kiss against the corner of Gerta's mouth as she did it, and Gerta felt her insides go warm, as if she'd drunk a cup of hot tea and it had burned all the way down.

It took them five days to reach the Snow Queen's palace. Five days of walking on the reindeer road, surrounded by ghosts, and five nights of being cut alive from the hide. Five nights of lying next to Janna in the dark and dreaming of the plants that slept beneath the snow.

The short Arctic day was nearly over when they saw a dark shape on the horizon.

The reindeer road swerved away from that darkness, swerved hard and final. Around Gerta's shoulders, the ghosts whispered to each other—*danger the queen of snows lives here danger run run run*—and she listened to them because they were the herd, until Mousebones cawed a warning and woke her.

Here. This is it. This is the Snow Queen's home.

There were no threads bleeding off where other reindeer had beaten a path to the human world. Gerta realized this almost too late and had to shoulder her way through the kindly ghosts and jump.

A thread drifted after her, one reindeer's worth of a path. *Which I suppose will make it easier for the next one to walk this road...*

This did not help her very much.

She knew in mid-air that the jump was bad, that the distance had twisted somehow. She landed it, barely, but the shock went up through her hooves and rattled her teeth and her antlers and left her breathless.

The sled slammed down hard on one runner, then the other. Janna squawked and overbalanced, falling hard. Gerta froze, trying to stop—what if the sled went over Janna?—and the sled slammed into the back of her legs and they folded up and she really did fall over, tangled in the traces.

She kicked, hard, in a panic, and then the human part of her panicked even harder *oh god oh god did I kick Janna or Mousebones oh god stop* and the panic bled to the reindeer body, which tried to kick again.

"Whoa!" said Janna. "Whoa! It's all right, Gerta, easy. Are you hurt—no, that's stupid, you couldn't tell me if you were—careful, love, careful—"

Gerta tried to listen but it was hard. Being on her side was bad and she couldn't run and her legs were tangled and if she just *kicked,* she could get loose, *surely* she could get loose—

"Easy…easy… I'm going to cut you out of the skin now…"

"Be a human for a bit," advised Mousebones, as if it were that were an easy thing to be.

Gerta closed her eyes and tried to be human. Then Janna touched her and she couldn't run and something had her and she kicked again, as hard as she could, and her hooves struck wood and—

"Easy…" crooned Janna. "Easy…"

What was it to be human? Gerta tried to remember and for some reason all she could think of was the dried fish jerky and the taste of salt. Salt was the thing that humans had that they gave you if you were good—

no, no, that's the wrong way around, you're not *a reindeer you're a human in a reindeer skin*

The cut was deeper and slower and hurt more than it had at any time in the last five days. Janna's angle was bad. Gerta rolled out of the skin, gasping, and blood ran in thin sheets from a gash across her collarbone.

"Are you all right?" said Janna. "Other than me being clumsy— shit—I'm sorry—"

Gerta nodded. Words would take a minute. She held snow against the cut, while Janna untangled the traces from around her ankles. She still had an urge to kick and try to run, but it was ebbing away.

Janna was working on her knees, not standing, and Gerta could see that she was favoring one leg. She did not stand up, but hitched herself along the ground to the sled and pulled out Gerta's cloak.

When Gerta could speak again, her first words were, "Did I hurt you?"

"Not you," said Janna. "The stupid sled tipped up and spilled me out." She smiled ruefully and thumped her ankle. "It's not broken, I don't think. I may have an exciting time walking for a bit."

Gerta winced.

"Oh, it's fine," said Janna. She grinned. "We're a pair, aren't we? Me with my ankle and you bleeding all over the snow. Help me wrap it and then we'll deal with *that.*"

She gestured, and for the first time Gerta looked up, ahead.

The darkness on the horizon was far closer. Their leap from the reindeer road had spanned a great deal more distance than she had thought.

No wonder I landed so hard. Thank goodness I didn't get any farther...we would have been torn to ribbons...

It rose thirty feet in the air, a wall of black lines rimed with frost. Great blades of thorns stabbed the air and crossed and recrossed so many times that it made a landscape of knives before them.

They had come, at last, to the fortress of the Snow Queen.

And Gerta had not the slightest idea how they were going to get in.

Chapter Thirty-Two

They wrapped up Janna's ankle and stuffed it back in her boot. "Before the swelling gets out of control," she said. "We'll have to cut the boot off at some point, probably, but I've got other things to worry about first."

"You sound awfully cheerful about this," said Gerta.

Janna laughed. "I do, don't I? I was trained as a horse-leech, and then as a healer, since we had more men than horses. So I at least *understand* this, unlike…oh, reindeer skins and women who gossip with swans." She nodded to her ankle. "This, at least, I can *fix.*"

Gerta laughed, and the sound of it surprised her. She had gotten used to the sound of reindeer laughter. The surprise of it made her laugh more, and then she couldn't stop, and then Janna was laughing too, and Gerta fell over on her back in the snow, giggling, because they were sitting in the snow in front of a terrifying hedge of frozen thorns and for some reason this was *hilarious.*

"Humans are all utterly mad," Mousebones observed dispassionately, which only made Gerta laugh harder.

"All right," said Janna weakly, wiping her eyes. "All right. Okay. I suppose we should go and see what sort of mess we're in."

"Yeah," said Gerta. She helped Janna to her feet. "Yeah, I suppose."

Janna leaned on her shoulder and hopped.

They made their slow way to the wall of thorns. It cast long blue shadows over the snow, but it stopped the wind, and so for a moment standing under the thorns felt warm.

It might have been a raspberry thicket once, if raspberries grew as high as houses. Ice glazed every stem. There were only a few leaves, tucked deep into the wall.

"The ice struck in fall or winter," said Janna, looking at the leaves.

"Or a hard wind came through first," said Gerta. She stretched out her fingers and touched the wall.

Ice melted away under her fingers. It took a little time, for she was no longer as warm as a reindeer. But eventually the thin glaze of ice was gone, and she touched bare stem.

It, too, was cold.

Well, what did I expect? The Snow Queen is old, and this wall has been frozen since Gran Aischa's day at least...

Up close, the gaps in the wall were larger. Gerta saw a few where she might have been able to squeak through, at least for a few feet. But the gaps were hardly paths and they might close up anywhere, and then she would have had to squirm back out, probably backwards, because there would be no room to turn around.

Janna exhaled slowly. "We're not getting through here," she said. "Maybe there's a way in somewhere..."

The wall seemed to run clear to the horizon in both directions. Gerta shook her head.

"I could walk along it, "she said doubtfully. "Or put on the hide and run. But it's miles long, at least."

"Awk!" said Mousebones. "It's a shame you don't have a helpful raven with you. You know, with *wings*. Who can *fly.*"

Gerta laughed, suddenly relieved. "Sorry, Mousebones. I'm an idiot. Can you find us a way in?"

Janna slapped her forehead. "Of course! Sorry, Mousebones. I should have thought."

"Yes, you should have. Awk!" He took to the air, dipped in the wind, and then flew south. His small black form was soon out of sight over the wall.

The humans went back to the sled, with Janna leaning on Gerta. For a moment, as she took the other girl's weight, Gerta felt physically powerful again, the way she had as a reindeer.

Which does me no good at all, if we can't get into the fortress...

The sled itself pulled fairly easily, even if one were a human. Gerta hauled it herself backward, over the snow, until they were back in the wind shadow of the thorn wall. Janna knelt and scraped the snow away, down to bare earth, then built a tiny fire.

"I'm glad there's dirt there," said Gerta.

Janna nodded. "I was afraid there might only be ice," she admitted. "Which doesn't make tea very well."

They sat on the sled together with the tent raised over them, watching the water heat for tea.

"So what do we do when we get inside?" asked Janna finally.

Gerta took a deep breath and let it out again, feeling as if it were coming from her toes. "I don't know," she said. "Find Kay. Bring him back out with us."

"And the Snow Queen?"

Gerta stared at her hands.

"I will assume by your silence that we *don't* have a plan."

"I still don't even know what she is," said Gerta wearily. "A spirit, I guess? Nobody knows anything about her. Maybe she'll kill me immediately. Maybe if we ask nicely, she'll just let Kay go."

"We'll start with that," said Janna, taking her hand and twining their fingers together. "After that, I suppose we'll just have to improvise."

"I had thought—maybe—if all else fails, I could turn into a reindeer and try to trample her?"

Janna bit her upper lip, obviously holding back laughter. "Well, it's better than anything else we've got."

The water began to steam gently. The wind howled overhead.

"I didn't know you were a horse-leech," said Gerta. "I should have guessed, with the way you were rescuing pigeons."

Janna nodded. "My father's band had horses once. But horses are expensive and men are cheap, and my father wanted me to learn something useful, since I was a girl and couldn't take over the band."

"Why couldn't you?" asked Gerta.

Janna snorted. "Women who run bandit troops have to be twice as smart and three times as vicious. I didn't want to deal with that. And I was not particularly interested in killing people and taking their money, anyway."

"Don't think I'm not grateful," said Gerta, and Janna laughed. "So you took up healing instead?"

"More or less. A real healer would laugh me out of the room, I'm sure." Janna shrugged. "Our horse-leech was an old man named Reckhardt. He taught me most of what he knew about healing humans and horses both." She added another chip of dried reindeer dung to the fire. "When you get down to it, humans are easier. Horses are made of legs, the way that birds are made of wings, and when something goes wrong with them, they're so hard to fix. And you can't explain that something's for their own good, either." She considered for a moment, then added, "Also, humans don't founder."

The tea was as warm as it was likely to get. Gerta poured it out for both of them.

Janna wrapped her fingers around her mug. "Anyway. Reckhardt wasn't a good man, but he was a kind one, if that makes any sense. It's hard to do anything with animals if you can't be kind. And he did his best." She stared into her tea.

Gerta tried to imagine growing up in a bandit cave, surrounded by killers and thieves, and could not. She leaned her shoulder against Janna's, and Janna leaned back.

"Why did I never ask you about your life before?" asked Gerta, surprised at herself.

"We've been busy this last week or so," said Janna dryly. "And also you've been a reindeer for large chunks of it. You?"

"Oh…" Gerta felt again that strange dislocation, as if her grandmother and her home and Kay were creatures from a fairy tale that someone had told her long ago. "Oh. I live…lived…with my grandmother. My father's dead. My mother's…um, she visits sometimes, but she married again and it was a small house. You know. And my grandmother needed somebody to help out. Well." She frowned down at her tea. "She didn't really, I don't think. And her best friend was Kay's grandmother, who's right across the alley, and his parents all live in the rooms there, and so did he, at least before…" She made a vague hand gesture that started somewhere south and ended up at the thorn wall before them. "Grandmother does weaving. She's good at it. She sells it. I was supposed to learn it, so I'd have a trade. I suppose I'm all right, but no one would pay for it."

She laughed a little at that. She hadn't so much as thought of a loom or a shuttle in weeks. It seemed so odd to consider going back, after all this, and sitting down in front of the loom and trying to start up again.

"How am I ever going to go back?" she said out loud. "Even if we find Kay—*when* we find him—I'll go home and say, 'Hi, sorry, I was gone for a year but I was enchanted for part of it and then I was a reindeer but not any more and by the way, I can talk to ravens now. But I brought Kay back.'"

She closed her teeth with a click but her thoughts ran on, unimpeded: *And also I don't actually think I want to marry him any more and I think I may be in love with a bandit girl who's killed at least one person that I know of, and why did none of you tell me that I could fall in love with a girl, anyway?*

"Perhaps they'll be so glad that you're home that they won't notice the rest," said Janna. Her voice sounded forced.

"My grandmother will like you," said Gerta.

Janna gave her an odd look. "You plan on taking a bandit home to meet your grandmother?"

"I assume you won't try to nick the silverware," said Gerta dryly.

"It's not that," said Janna quietly. "You know that."

Gerta took a deep breath.

She knew that it was stupid to trust a bandit and an admitted murderer.

She knew that they had met under dreadful circumstances and those circumstances had gotten steadily worse.

But she also knew that she trusted Janna. Something had happened in those days and nights on the reindeer road, something to do with sharp knives, with hide and herd and things that humans did not have words for.

She would trust Janna to the ends of the earth. And that was good, because that was where they were standing.

"It will be all right," Gerta said, and meant it.

Janna gripped her hand. Before she could say anything, they heard a familiar caw. Mousebones landed on the sled, shaking out his bad wing. "It's too cold," he said. "My wing's not happy with this."

Janna built up the fire a little and the raven hopped down next to it, stretching his wing out to soak up the little heat.

The wind howled overhead, and it smelled metallic, like fresh snow.

What will happen if it snows while we're sitting out here? How long will our food hold out?

"Well?" said Gerta, when she could wait no longer. "Did you find a way in?"

Mousebones snapped his beak. "Aurk! Of course I did."

Chapter Thirty-Three

The way in was farther than Janna could hop. They had to go back through the long weary process of transformation and harnessing. Janna apologized and Gerta brushed it aside.

"If I couldn't walk, we'd find a way," she said, and threw the reindeer hide around her shoulders.

They stayed in the wind-shadow of the thorns as they went. Gerta was sweating by the time Mousebones called a halt.

The entryway was very low, only about three feet tall. The thorns grew over the top, but the snow beneath had been hollowed out in a long, curving run. It was slick and compacted in the center, beaten into murky blue ice.

The trail of blue ice continued out from the thorns and over the landscape. Gerta turned and pulled the sled alongside it, away from the thorn wall, to see where it went.

She had not gone far at all before she smelled minerals and saw steam rising in the air.

The ice gave way to mud, and the mud to fantastically colored water. They were ridiculously bright in that landscape of black and white and grey—turquoise and orange in concentric rings and a pungent smell of rotting eggs.

"It's a hot spring!" said Janna. "Something's coming out of the thorns to use the hot spring. But what would do that?"

Mousebones hopped over to a small, steaming mud puddle and held his wing out over it. "Ahhh...that's the stuff."

It's the otters, Gerta wanted to say. *That's a giant otter slide.*

She'd seen them in winter, near her village. When everyone bundled up and went out to throw snowballs, or to ice fish or check the trap lines, you'd find otters playing on every snowbank, sliding down over and over, until their bellies beat the snow into glossy ice. Then they loved it even more.

She nudged Mousebones with her nose and the raven hopped to one side, grumbling. "What is it?"

The otters can fly. Why are they sliding down here if they can fly?

The raven cocked his head at her skeptically. "You don't know otters very well, do you?"

Gerta regretted that reindeers have little concept of sarcasm. She snorted instead.

"Ravens can fly, too. We still slide sometimes. Sliding is fun," said Mousebones. He tucked in his wing, flopped over in the snow, and rolled. Janna laughed.

Gerta gave an exaggerated reindeer nod and turned the sled around. She trotted back along the length of the slide and stood, waiting for the knife.

When she had climbed out from under the hide, she told Janna about the otters.

"I'd forgotten the otters," said Janna. "Very well, I can see it." She reached out a fingertip and ran it down Gerta's throat. "You...ah. It's scarring, a little. There's all these white lines. Like cat scratches, only...not."

Gerta swallowed hard, as much from the touch as the idea of the scars. "Well. I suppose they'll fade eventually."

"I suppose."

They stepped apart. Janna eyed the low, slick tunnel with dismay. "My ankle won't hold up to that."

"It's too low to take the sled in," said Gerta. "I suppose we'll have to crawl."

"My ankle's going to love this," muttered Janna. "Very well! Lead on."

They left the sled and put on packs. Gerta tied the reindeer hide to herself like a strange cape, upside down with the pack between them. The reindeer antlers bounced and gouged long lines in the ice on either side of her hips, but she did not know how else to manage them, and she did not dare leave it behind.

On hands and knees, they entered the tunnel.

It was not quite as bad as Gerta had feared. The slope was very gentle, and the edges of the slide were not completely beaten into ice. If she stayed to one side and dug her gloved hands into the snow there, she could make manage a sort of slithery crawl.

The light under the thorn wall was blue-green and dim, and came as much from the snow itself as from the sky. Black scribbles of stems closed overhead. It was impossible to tell if they were branches or roots or both.

Mousebones flew past them, a series of hops. Occasionally he would tuck himself into a feathery black oval and slide down the ice on his back, snickering in raven-fashion.

"They do that on steep rooftops sometimes," said Janna. "When our winter quarters were over near the coast, I'd see them doing that on the stable roof. It always looked like fun."

She sounded wistful. Gerta glanced back over her shoulder, but the light was too poor to make out her expression.

"What was the coast like?" asked Gerta. "I've never seen the sea."

Janna was silent for a moment. Her breathing was magnified by the tunnel, and lit echoes all around them. "The sea is very large," she said finally. "And it's not like anything but itself. I can't explain it. I liked living there, though."

"I would like to see it," said Gerta.

"It is very much worth seeing."

They kept sliding. Gerta's knees and palms ached with cold, even through her heavy clothes. She was very aware of the way that her knees went together, the joint and the tendon and the kneecap sliding over both and taking the brunt of the ice.

"How is your ankle?"

"It's felt better."

Mousebones went by them again on his back.

"By the way," he called, as he slid past, "you're almost there."

"I get the impression he is not taking this seriously," said Janna.

Gerta would have said something, but the roof of the tunnel slanted upward abruptly.

She blinked up, into bright light, and the interested faces of a half-dozen bone-white otters.

Chapter Thirty-Four

"It's a human!"

"It smells like a dead reindeer."

"It's got a dead reindeer on it. Sort of upside down."

The otters had peculiar voices, deep but squeaky. Gerta didn't know whether to laugh or try to run away.

"It smells like both."

"Perhaps it's like a centaur. Only the front is a human and the bottom is a dead reindeer."

The other otters turned and stared very hard at that one, which looked abashed. "What?"

Janna poked her head up through the tunnel entrance beside Gerta. "I can understand them…" she said wonderingly.

The otters seized on this immediately.

"Of course you can.

"We speak human very well."

"We speak several human languages."

"*Suohtas duinna deaivvadit.*"

"*Hyvää huomenta!*"

"*Sprichst du auch Deutsch?*"

"*Diné bizaadísh dinits'a'?*"

Gerta looked at Janna helplessly. Janna shook her head. "Maybe if you spoke a lot slower…" she said.

"Oh, never mind."

"We speak this one fine."

"We learned a lot of languages."

"It's not like Herself was going to learn *our* language."

"She said it was undignified. Just because there was chittering."

"And smells."

"Musk is very expressive."

"Some people don't appreciate musk nearly enough."

"So we learned her language."

"Not that we had much choice."

"It was that or be blasted with the wrath of a thousand blizzards."

"Or whatever she was going to blast us with."

"Anyway, we like languages."

"Words are like fish and you catch them and you get to keep them forever."

"And some of Herself's toys teach us their words. Before they freeze."

Gerta inhaled sharply.

They were talking about Kay. They had to be talking about Kay.

…or they're talking about the one after Kay. Or the one after that. You slept for seven months, while he was freezing.

She kept her voice as steady as she could and said "Does she have one now?"

"Oh, lots!"

"She means an unfrozen one."

"Well, she should have *said.*"

"It takes them ages to freeze."

"There's one."

"She only keeps one unfrozen one at a time."

"She is strictly monogamous that way."

"Like a praying mantis made out of ice."

"Oh, very nice image."

"I came up with that years ago."

"You did *not.*"

"You're always taking credit for things."

Janna and Gerta exchanged looks. "When did they ever see a praying mantis?" asked Janna.

"Sometimes Herself likes toys from very far south."

"One explained praying mantises to us."

"He drew a picture."

"He was always drawing pictures."

"Then he froze and he stopped drawing pictures."

"About the unfrozen one…" said Gerta.

"He's still unfrozen."

"He doesn't speak any languages we don't know, though."

"And he never draws any pictures."

"He's pretty boring."

"He sits in one room and does puzzles."

Gerta's heart squeezed. *It must be Kay. It* must *be.*

"Could you take me—?" she began, but Janna held up a hand.

"Is…Herself…here now?" the bandit girl asked.

"Of course."

"She hardly ever leaves without her sled."

"Sometimes she walks around the hedge."

Gerta and Janna exchanged looks.

"Well," said Janna quietly. "I suppose we will get to improvise after all."

Gerta said "Can you take me to the unfrozen boy?"

One of the otters shrugged. It was a long, fascinating ripple that started somewhere in the neck and continued all the way to the tail. "I suppose."

She—Gerta was nearly certain it was a she—leaned down into the hole and opened her jaws. Gerta had a moment of panic. The otter was narrower in the chest than a reindeer, but a great deal longer.

Oh god, they're basically giant playful wolverines…

The otter grabbed Gerta's collar in her teeth and flipped her out as neatly as a regular-sized otter grabbing a fish. Gerta landed upside down and narrowly avoided impaling herself on the trailing reindeer antlers.

Another otter dipped its head into the tunnel and flipped Janna out the same way. Janna landed with a yelp.

When Gerta stopped seeing stars, she sat up and looked around.

The room was enormous. The ceiling was lost in swirling winds, like a distant snowstorm. The walls were made of ice. The floor was made of ice as well, but the branches of the thorn hedge had grown into it, so it was ice shot through with blackness.

In one corner of the room was an enormous pile of fish, frozen solid. In another was a nest as big as the house Gerta grew up in. It had apparently started life as silken pillows, but the otters had gutted the cushions and it was now a pile of frosty feathers and long rags of sky-blue silk.

Mousebones flew up out of the tunnel and landed well out of reach of the otters, who were instantly fascinated.

"A raven!"

"We speak Raven!"

"Ark! Ark! Ark!"

"That is not speaking Raven," said Mousebones severely. "That is saying 'Ark' and you are saying it badly."

"Can you fly, raven?"

"Of course I can fly!" said Mousebones.

"So can we!"

"When Herself hitches us up to her sled."

"Then we fly like ravens."

"No, we don't. We fly like clouds. We don't flap."

"Flapping would be undignified."

"It would be if you lot did it," agreed Mousebones. "Otters aren't made to flap."

"Do you have a name?"

"Ravens always have the best names."

"They're so long and they take them so seriously."

Mousebones looked offended. "I have an excellent name and I don't think I will tell you what it is if you're going to act like that."

"Oh, don't be like that."

"We'll tell you our names."

"We will."

They sat up, one after another, with their tails wrapped over their feet like cats.

"Glint."

"Glitter."

"Ur."

"Frost-eyes."

"Misting."

"Fish-eater."

The raven looked unimpressed. "Typical. And short."

"We have to take them off sometimes."

"Sometimes we trade them with each other."

"It's easier when they're shorter."

"Tell us yours."

"I am The Sound Of Mousebones Crunching Under The Hooves Of God," said Mousebones.

(Gerta translated this exchange in an undertone for Janna. "Good lord," said the bandit girl. "They could talk the legs off a wooden goat.")

"Ooooh!"

"That is an *excellent* name."

"I want a name like that."

"But taking off a name like that would take so *long*."

"I do not intend to take it off," said Mousebones. "I may even add to it. I believe that after this mad adventure into the north, I shall be The Sound Of *Frozen* Mousebones Crunching Under The Hooves Of God. Assuming that I am not dead, which requires a different sort of name."

Gerta translated this as well, and Janna cleared her throat. "On that topic, we would like to prevent dying if possible. Can we find Gerta's friend and leave?"

The otter who had identified herself as Ur—Gerta thought it was the one who had pulled her out of the tunnel, but it was very hard to tell—said "Oh. Right. The unfrozen one."

She turned and padded across the floor. Gerta and Janna hurried after her. Janna leaned on Gerta's shoulder.

"He's boring," called Glitter after them.

"We are much more interesting."

"We would trade names with you, if you like."

"Maybe later," called Gerta. It wouldn't do to get on the otters' bad side. They were playful and cheerful and their teeth were longer than human fingers.

"We shall see you later, then."

"Báhcet dearvan."

"Come back and talk to us."

"We have fish."

"It is excellent fish."

"We should have fish now."

"Yes."

Mousebones cast a longing glance behind them as the white otters fell on the pile of fish as if they were starving.

Ur led them out an archway and up a flight of stairs. Everything was made of ice. Gerta had never known there were so many colors of ice—deep greens and metallic blues and silvers.

Everything was very silent except for the sound of the wind rushing overhead. Their footsteps barely made any sound, and the antler points on the reindeer's head dragged on the ice like the poles of a travois, a thin little scraping sound against the wind.

At the top of the stairs lay an immense corridor, which opened into an even more immense hall. Pillars of ice held up a ceiling so distant that Gerta began to think that the otter's den, which had seemed so huge, was actually rather small compared to the rest of the palace.

They exited the hall by a doorway that would not have been out of place as the entry to a cathedral, but which seemed unobtrusive.

Then another hall and another door and another, all unmarked, all glazed in frost.

"I'm glad we have a guide," said Janna quietly. "We could wander in this place for days. Until we starved, or froze."

"People have," said Ur. "Sometimes Herself's toys decide they don't want to be here. They almost never find the way out, though."

She paused, as if waiting for another otter to say something, and then seemed to remember that she was the only one there. "We tell them, if they ask us. One or two left. But then she gets upset and there is no fish. And sometimes she freezes their hearts. Then they don't try to leave any more." She gave another of her long, rippling shrugs.

"Does that kill them?"

"Oh, no. Humans are fine if their hearts freeze. They can keep moving for years like that."

"Can you take us by a way that will avoid Herself? We…ah… don't want to bother her," said Gerta. The otters did not actually seem to like the Snow Queen very much, but she didn't want to push her luck.

Ur flicked her tail, like a large cat. "I'll do my best," she said, sounding a bit dry, and Gerta thought that perhaps the question hadn't been as subtle as she thought.

They entered yet another hallway. This one was reflective ice, and made a vast, distorted mirror of the walls. Ur became three giant white otters, weaseling along in unison.

Gerta looked at her own reflection and recoiled.

"Oh…" she said softly.

It was stupid. She had not worried what she looked like for many days now. It did not matter. She only needed to find Kay.

But the girl in the mirror was a wild, ragged thing, her hair straggling under the fur cap that Livli had given her. There were dark circles under her eyes and smears of dirt. The reindeer hide hung lumpy and bunched and the dead head lolled behind her.

She could not think for a moment, what the pattern on the front of her tunic was, and then she realized that it was long rivulets of dried blood, where the cuts on her neck had dripped and healed and dripped again.

She thought, *No wonder Janna does not want me right now. I look like a madwoman.*

Oh, I am being so stupid! I should not care. We are going to face a great enemy. It doesn't matter what my hair looks like.

And then, a long moment later, she thought, *What will Kay think?*

Gerta knew that he *should* be grateful for rescue, for any rescue, but she remembered Kay. Kay who loved snow because it was clean. And she would appear, filthy and stained and stinking of dead reindeer, and he would think…what?

She was surprised to feel a spark of irritation at the Kay in her imagination and had to shake her head at herself. *Now I'm inventing slights with the person I'm here to rescue…*

"You should have told me I looked a sight," she said, struggling to laugh.

Janna gave her a puzzled look. "What?" And then she looked in the mirror and laughed, and said, "I'm hardly fit to call anyone a sight!"

Gerta looked at her, really looked, and saw that Janna, too, was ragged. Her dark skin was smudged with dirt and frost had formed on the brim of her hat. She was carrying a pack that was twice the size of Gerta's and was bent forward under the weight, and she was still limping on her bad ankle.

"I hadn't noticed," said Gerta.

"Well. Neither had I. Let's go back to not noticing."

They toiled after Ur in slightly better spirits. The otter waited for them at the end of the hall. Mousebones shook his head in avian disgust.

"Not much farther," said Ur.

They entered the next hall, and Gerta gasped. Mousebones dropped off her shoulder and flew forward, favoring his wing.

There was a figure leaning against a pillar.

Frost coated his skin and hair. He had a broad, pleasant face, despite his slight frown. His eyes were closed, and each eyelash was outlined in ice. His cheek was pressed against the pillar as if he had leaned against it to rest and never moved again.

He looked to be about sixteen years old.

"Don't mind him," said Ur. "He's been frozen for years. Fish-Eater wasn't even weaned when Herself brought him here."

This would have been a more useful statement if Gerta had any idea how long a giant otter lived.

It was hard to turn her back on the frozen boy. She was not sure if it was out of fear that he would move, or pity for the unburied dead.

Is he dead, though?

She looked over her shoulder. He had not moved.

"We can't save them all," said Janna. "I don't know if we'll even save ourselves." Gerta nodded.

She was not sorry to leave the hall behind.

They passed two more, on the way to wherever they were going. Both had their eyes closed. Gerta was glad of that. It would have been much worse if their eyes had been open.

"That was the one who painted," said Ur, of an olive-skinned young man clad in bright blue. "We liked him. But she promised him the secret to painting all the colors of ice, and he stayed too long."

Gerta had never thought about the difficulty of painting ice. It seemed an odd thing to stay and freeze to death over, even so.

"Artists are odd," said Mousebones, walking around the man in blue. "Even for humans."

Janna leaned on her a little less as they walked. "Feeling any better?" asked Gerta.

The bandit girl's lips quirked. "My feet are cold enough that the ankle doesn't hurt as badly. That's not a good thing, but at the moment, I'll take it."

Gerta was looking over at Janna when she said that, and so it took her a moment realize that the click of Ur's claws on the ice stopped.

She looked up.

They stood on a balcony overlooking a swirling snowstorm. Before them, six feet high and twice that wide, were pieces of ice seemingly hanging suspended in the air.

She understood suddenly how the painter had been trapped. The ice crystals had grown into fantastical shapes, beautiful as flowers, sharp as swords. They shone a thousand colors of blue and violet and silver, rippling with reflected light.

In front of the ice, with his back to them, stood Kay.

Chapter Thirty-Five

"Kay!" said Gerta. Her voice came out too quiet, as if she was in a dream where she could not yell for help. She took a deeper breath. "Kay!"

He turned.

He was a little taller than she remembered, and his shoulders a little broader. He wore a white jacket and fur-lined boots. The seasons that had passed had been kinder to him than to her, except that his skin was very pale.

He looked from the otter to Janna and then to Gerta without a trace of recognition, and his eyebrows drew down, as if they were interrupting him.

"It's me," said Gerta. "Gerta, I mean. I came to find you."

"Gerta?" said Kay. His voice sounded exactly the same as it always had.

He stared at her and said, "You look *terrible.*"

The spark of irritation that Gerta had felt before flared up and became a stab. "I'm here to rescue you!" she said.

"I don't need rescuing," said Kay. He waved to the crystals hanging behind him. "I'm working."

Janna made a small sound of disbelief. Gerta looked over at her and the bandit girl shook her head ruefully. "Well, I didn't see that coming," she said.

Gerta rubbed her hands over her face.

She had been expecting to find Kay, perhaps hungry and half-frozen, in a cell somewhere. She had expected an icy jailbreak, an escape through the halls, and, if they were unlucky, a confrontation with the Snow Queen.

She hadn't expected that he wouldn't want to come with them.

"Is that a *dead reindeer?*" asked Kay. "Why are you dragging a dead reindeer around?"

"It's complicated," said Gerta wearily.

"This is going well," said Mousebones.

"And you've got a crow," said Kay.

Mousebones gave him a look of withering disgust. "Crow? *Crow?* Are you *sure* you want to rescue him?"

Ur scratched her ear. "His heart's frozen," she said.

"Oh!" said Gerta. This was a relief. Obviously Kay was acting strangely, obviously it was the Snow Queen's fault. "Can we thaw his heart?"

"I suppose you could roast it," said Ur doubtfully.

Mousebones snickered. Janna said, "That's…not as helpful as it could be."

"Oh. Sorry."

"You don't need to talk about me like I'm not here," said Kay. "My heart is fine." He turned his back and put his hands into the strange array of ice crystals again.

"What is that you're working on?" asked Gerta.

"A puzzle," said Kay. "*The* puzzle. The final one. If I can fit it all together, it will show me eternity."

"People say they want to see eternity, but it's really quite boring," said Mousebones. "It just goes on and on, you know."

Gerta looked at Janna helplessly. "What do we do now?"

"I could hit him over the head," said Janna. "He might die, though, so I don't recommend it. But once he's out, we could turn you into a reindeer and hog-tie him and then leave."

Kay made a disgusted noise, not looking at them. "This is the worst rescue attempt I've ever heard of. I don't need rescuing anyway, and even if I did, I could do it better myself. If you don't know what you're doing, go away. And maybe clean up too. You look a fright."

"On second thought, a good blow to the head might be just what he requires," said Janna.

Gerta put her face in her hands. "Your family's really worried," she said hopelessly.

For the first time, Kay faltered. He turned his head, with his fingers still full of ice. "Are they?"

"Your grandmother took to her bed. She might be dead by now. I don't know."

"Oh," said Kay. He frowned, but then his face smoothed. "Well, you can go back and tell them that I'm fine. I'm doing very important work. They'll be happy to know that."

"They won't be happy until you come home," said Gerta desperately, feeling the moment slipping away.

He turned back to the crystals. "They'll have to be. I can't leave this. I'm close to solving it."

"But if you stay here, you'll freeze to death! Like all the others!"

He hitched up one shoulder, not looking at her. "Then I'll freeze. If I can solve this and see the shape of eternity, it's worth it."

"What a load of bollocks," remarked Janna, to no one in particular.

"Awk," agreed Mousebones.

Gerta started to say something—anything—and then she saw Kay pick up a jagged crystal and move it. The edges sliced into his flesh as if he'd grabbed a naked blade…and nothing happened.

There was no blood. There was only a thin pink line across his white, white fingers.

Fingers that, she saw now, were crossed and re-crossed with hundreds of pink lines.

If he cannot even feel pain, how did I think he'd feel love or gratitude or guilt or anything else?

Gerta clutched the reindeer hide. It was warm under her fingers, and steadied her a little. She could feel the pulse of the reindeer road in it, and even if she could not reach it, she knew that it existed. There was one place in the world where time went in all directions and the herd moved together as one.

She wanted to cry or scream or demand that Kay go with them, but none of those things would help. Therefore she must move in the next direction, whatever that may be.

She straightened.

Gerta did not pretend to know what made someone live, but she knew that a person with a frozen heart, who could slice themselves to ribbons and not bleed, was in a fair way to not being alive any longer.

She turned to Janna and leaned over and whispered "Hit him over the head. We'll just have to risk it."

Janna nodded.

And what might have happened next, no one would ever know, because the doorway behind them filled with frost, and a high, shattering voice said, "What has come into my kingdom?"

Chapter Thirty-Six

The voice was not human. That was the thing that struck Gerta first. It was not human, nor even close to human, no matter what the Snow Queen chose to look like. The vowels were the shrill complaint of frozen metal and the consonants were the crackle of breaking ice. No human born could have a voice like that.

Gerta turned, and the Snow Queen stood in the doorway.

She was very tall and very pale and very beautiful. She wore a robe of white, trimmed in ermine fur, and the fur glittered under a glaze of frost.

She looked at Kay, and he gazed back at her and a light came into Kay's face like none Gerta had ever seen, and he said, "I've almost got it."

The Snow Queen turned her head, and the first thing that Gerta felt was gratitude that she had not looked at Gerta, and the second was a stab of shame, because her eye fell on Janna instead.

Janna staggered.

Her face went slack and her eyes went wide. She let out a tiny moan and Gerta *knew* what she was seeing reflected in the Snow Queen's eyes. The worst of herself, the messy mortal bloody bits, filthy and stinking and small and weak and unworthy and *how dare she look that way at Janna?*

Rage rose up in Gerta's heart, as hot and red as the ice palace was cold and blue. She launched herself across the room, away from Kay, thinking of nothing except that no one, *no one*, should ever think such thoughts about Janna.

Her shoulder struck the Snow Queen and it was like falling against a shelf full of glass jars—the hard interspersed with the shockingly brittle. Things shattered. The Queen's robe bucked strangely as the body under it broke apart and fell back.

What? What just happened?

Gerta stumbled forward, and Janna caught her. They staggered together as Janna's ankle buckled.

"I should have listened," gasped the bandit girl. "You told me, but I thought—well, if someone told you that you were foul, you'd believe it with all your heart, so I didn't realize—gods, how did you do that *twice?*"

"Are you all right?" said Gerta. "She shouldn't have looked at you like that!"

"What did you do?" cried Kay, standing over the Queen. "You broke her! You always break everything! Can't I ever do anything without you chasing me?"

Gerta gaped at him. Janna hissed.

"This is why you don't mate with your nestmates," said Mousebones pragmatically. "It's always 'Oh, yes, and remember the time you ate that cricket that I was supposed to get?' for the rest of your life." He paused, and then added, "Well, that and the inbreeding."

Ur, who had taken herself off to the corner and was staying well out of the fray, made an indelicate sound.

The Snow Queen rose.

She did not stand up like a human, she simply rose up from the floor as if remaking herself from the material of the palace. Which, thought Gerta, given that she was apparently made of ice, seemed very likely.

Kay's face shone and he reached out to the Queen with both hands. She took them in hers and Gerta could not tell where one set of white, bloodless fingers left off and the other began.

Then she swung her head, narrow and sharp as an Arctic fox, toward the girls.

Gerta stepped forward and pushed Janna back. Janna made a noise of protest, but her ankle buckled as she tried to push back, and so it was Gerta who took the full force of the Queen's gaze.

She was nothing and no one, she was the wretched child of a wretched race, short-lived and bedraggled, with her hair in knots and blood staining the front of her clothes. She was half an animal and no one could have loved a creature such as she.

She could not think, not in human words. Her mind was empty of anything but horror.

She sank down to her knees, and the Snow Queen's gaze sank with her, driving her to the floor. The Queen's eyes were vast mirrors and Gerta was a speck that had dared to marred the beauty of their surface.

The reindeer hide bunched around her as she fell, and in her reflection, she saw the antlers frame her face.

The hide had been a magnificent gift, however poorly she wore it.

The hide. The gift. The herd.

In the speech of reindeer, she found that she could think again. *I am here. I am still alive.*

If she was half an animal, let the animal half speak for her, then. The human part was tied up with human things like self-loathing, but that did not matter. There were no words in reindeer speech for *I hate myself.* It was not a concept that could be thought, and so she did not bother to think it.

She thought, instead, *the thing before me smells of snow.*

Janna was screaming, but she was screaming in the human language, and Gerta did not dare slip back into that.

Kay came toward her, with his face ominously blank, but then a black shape sliced between them and Mousebones drove his beak at Kay's face, cawing a raven's mobbing call, as if Kay were a hawk instead of a human boy. "Awk! Awk! You will *not!* Egg-stealer! Nest-thief!"

The thing that smelled of snow leaned forward. Her eyes narrowed.

She is expecting me to die, but I am not dead yet.

This angered the snow thing, and it raised its hands and brought them down, like a human with a whip. Reindeer knew whips, and Gerta's shoulders rose in anticipation of the blow.

Cold was coming up from her knees, where they were splayed awkwardly on the icy floor. The cold rose, as if she had stepped into an icy river, coming up her body, freezing her ribcage in mid-breath.

I must get warm—

The cold reached her face. The world went pale and blurred as her eyes froze and it got darker and darker, a long winter night without the hope of stars.

Only her heart was not frozen, and the last thing Gerta felt was it hammering in her chest, beating hopelessly against the cold.

Chapter Thirty-Seven

The thorns that surrounded the Snow Queen's fortress were old beyond telling, and they had slept for a long time.

The roots of the thorns were sunk deep, and many of them had died, but more were tangled in the warm mud around the hot springs. Perhaps even the Snow Queen did not know that they were still alive. The branches were brittle and rimed with ice, but throughout the thickest stems ran a thin, thin sliver of green.

There is nothing in the world so patient as a plant awaiting spring.

Gerta sank beneath the fortress in a dream that had no waking at the end of it. Her body was distant and useless and cold.

Underneath the fortress there was snow, and under the snow was earth and threading the earth were the roots of the wall of thorns.

Ah, thought Gerta. *I remember this.*

She reached out to the sleeping plants and they wrapped around her, more watchful than any plant that Gerta had spoken to before, for all that they were sleeping.

She tasted earth and water and the harsh minerals of the springs. Surprise. Puzzlement. It had been a long time since a living thing spoke to them. Someone had spoken to them long ago, and they had answered, but it had been long and long and long ago.

How long have you been here? asked Gerta.

Winter. The land was green and then ice came and covered everything. There had been ice before. Eventually the ice would melt, and there would be green, drowsy days under the pale northern sun.

How long has that been?

Confusion. Seasons follow seasons. One begins when another one ends. If spring had not begun, then winter had not ended.

It occurred to Gerta that the thorn hedge had a strong grasp of the seasons and no sense at all of time.

She would have laughed if her body had not been frozen somewhere far away. Of course. Of all the plants that she had touched since she left the witch's house, had any of them understood time?

I should hurry, she thought, and hard on the heels of that, *or perhaps I am dead and it doesn't matter anyway.*

Well. If she had already died, there was nothing to be done about it. For Mousebones and Janna and poor foolish Kay, however, she might yet do…something.

Tell me your dreams, said Gerta to the thorns.

They did.

The sun was kind and this was a good green land. Someone stood with her bare feet on the earth, someone that was not human. Gerta did not know what she was, but she was good and kind.

The kind woman stretched out her hands and asked.

The answer lay in growing. Wood pierced Gerta's flesh. Leaves swelled and broke across her skin. It hurt, like a stretch across sore muscles. She stretched farther and farther until she met herself in a circle, with the kind woman in the center.

She rose up, many feet high, branches curving inward like a secret, the old wood growing hard and brittle, the new shoots young and strong. Berries erupted from her. The kind woman reached up and picked them. That was good. That was correct. They were a gift from Gerta and the thorns to the woman who had asked them to grow.

Seasons chased one another. There were many. Snow fell on the brambles, only to melt again. Birds nested under the thorns, and ate the berries that grew there.

The thorns were glad. They could be generous. The birds were such small, fleeting things, but the thorns could feed them and make their short lives easier. Then the birds would spread the seeds far and wide, a gift given in exchange for a gift taken. Kindness fed kindness. It was good.

Then a storm came. A thing came walking inside it, a thing that was not good or kind. It touched the wall and spoke a word and the word was *winter.*

The thorns knew their place in the order of things. They settled down to sleep through the cold season.

It was only the deepest roots that were wakeful, and only they who felt the screaming of the kind woman, and the blood that melted away the snow and sank into the earth.

The thorn hedge drank in the trace of iron, the shudder of salt, and made them part of itself. It was the last gift that a plant could give to the one who raised it up.

And then it settled down, the green buried deep, to dream and wait for spring.

That is why you are so wakeful, said Gerta. *The blood of the kind woman, whatever she was.*

Agreement. Taste of iron.

Can you help me?

Puzzlement. Winter. Frost on the branches. Waiting.

No. I can't wait. Don't you understand? Spring is not going to come.

Disbelief.

The thing that came. The storm. That was the Snow Queen. While she is here, there will never be spring. Winter will never end and you will never grow again.

She did not think the thorns understood. Perhaps it was too alien a concept. She tried to shape a picture in her mind, of snow laying over the branches, the sun crossing the sky, over and over, winter unending, until at last the roots froze and the skeleton of the hedge stood held up by ice and spring never came.

Gerta tasted salt and ash, sudden and powerful. It choked her and she had no body to gag and clear it from her mouth.

It took her a moment to realize that was the only way that plants could express horror.

Of course…they can't grow in salt. Salt kills fields. Of course…

Winter never ends? asked the thorns.

Never.

No more birds in the branches? No more berries?

None. Unless you stop the Snow Queen. She tried to shape another image, of birds landing in the frozen hedge, birds with nothing to eat, birds starving and flying away again.

Salt. Ash. The smell of burning.

In the heart of the thorn hedge, something woke.

It felt like rage.

Gerta tried to fall back. The thorn hedge was too large, too old, too angry. Thousands of years of sleep had ended and transmuted into fury.

She could not escape. She was locked into the hedge as if she were a bird herself and the stems had grown up to trap her.

The roots dug deep and pulled warmth from the earth, sending it violently through the stems. Green shoots erupted in every direction, splitting the ice apart. The outer layers of green died as soon as the frost touched them, but were shoved forward by the growth behind them, like an army climbing over the bodies of its dead.

It felt to Gerta like thrusting her hands into a fire and trying to heal her flesh faster than it burned away, and yet somehow, agonizingly, she was doing it.

She screamed, or tried, but it was lost in the rage and the growth and the dying. She had nothing to scream with anyway. Her body was far away and there was only root and branch and thorn and ice, and the ice was shattering away.

The thorn hedge reached into the fortress and tore the white walls down.

Inside the walls was the thing made of storms. Gerta could see it, distantly, a thing that wore a human face to reflect the faces around it. It was a small thing. It brought cold, but there was no cold that could stand forever against the armies of spring.

The thing reached out and tried to speak *winter* to the hedge again, but the hedge was no longer listening.

Cracks shot through the halls of the Snow Queen's fortress, zig-zags that widened and deepened and split apart. Green tendrils grew out of them, withering to brown even as they grew, but the damage was done. Ice fell from the ceiling. Pillars toppled by themselves, or were overgrown with vines and thrown down.

From underneath the snow, under the frozen layer of earth, the roots heaved up stone and dirt. The foundations of the fortress split and whole wings fell, crumbling into drifts of rock and snow.

The hedge reached the room where the Snow Queen stood. Gerta saw herself, from the outside, lying stiffly in Janna's arms. Kay crouched down with his arms over his head. Mousebones was cawing.

And the Snow Queen stood there, calling storm, calling blizzard, shouting the name of winter over and over.

Thorns rose up and wrapped around her. They died at once, but the next rank was ready and the next, like a prison made of wicker, and it did not matter if the stems died as they wrapped around her for the hedge had a raging green heart.

The Snow Queen vanished under a hundred layers of leaves. And then the fortress began to fall apart in earnest, as the Queen pulled the cold toward her, trying desperately to gather enough power to freeze the hedge that bound her.

The voice at the heart of the thorns roared with triumph.

In the great growing maelstrom, Gerta could not imagine that anything would hear her, or listen, but she had to try.

Please! she said desperately. *Please let me go!*

She shaped the image as best she could, the bird trapped by stems, fluttering.

For a long, terrible time she thought that the rage of the thorns was too deep and that it could not hear her. It would tear the palace apart and never notice the tiny creatures within it.

Then—

Agreement. Kindness.

Birds in branches.

She felt herself gathered up. She could no longer see anything but leaves.

The taste of berries filled her mouth, and that must mean she had a mouth again, and then she was falling into a sleep that had no dreams inside it.

Chapter Thirty-Eight

Gerta woke feeling pleasantly warm for what felt like the first time in her life.

She was lying against something soft, and there were arms around her.

It was very comfortable. It was not quite as warm as a sauna, but it was pleasant. If she had not been developing a crick in her neck, she would have fallen asleep again.

She stretched and yawned and Janna said, "Please tell me that you're alive and that your brain wasn't blasted out of your head by whatever it was that happened."

Gerta laughed and then her mouth filled up with water and she spluttered. She had to cough and Janna pounded her back enthusiastically until she could breathe again.

They were in the hot spring, in one of the pools near the edge. It was bathwater warm. "You still had a heartbeat," said Janna, "but you were freezing. I was afraid if I dropped you straight into the hottest pool, the shock would kill you, so we built a fire until you warmed up a bit, and then into the pool. I didn't know what else to do."

"It's fine," said Gerta. She tested each finger and toe. They all moved, although not without some complaining. "I think I'm okay. But what happened?"

"You tell me," said Janna, and turned her gently to look back across the snow.

The thorn hedge had fallen inward. Green stems as thick as Gerta's leg snaked across a mound of buckled earth and jumbled stone.

"Was that the fortress?" asked Gerta.

Janna nodded. "After you froze, things got very strange. Your friend was yelling and—ah—well, anyway the Queen just stood there, and then all of a sudden the place was falling down. The bottom came up and the ceiling fell in and there were vines everywhere. It was a mess. I assume you had something to do with it."

It was the otters that had saved them, Janna explained. They had pulled the humans out of the falling fortress, swapping jokes the entire time, with Mousebones leading the way.

"And Kay?"

Janna looked sheepish. "Oh. I—ah—may have punched your friend in the face."

Gerta put her hand over her mouth.

"He was coming at you after you knocked the Queen down! And Mousebones held him off, but...well." She coughed. "He made it out, anyway. His hands are a wreck. I bandaged them up, but he's gone a bit odd. You'll see."

There was a fire burning off to the right. Gerta could see the humped shapes of the otters, and—two figures?

"They brought one of the other boys out," said Janna. "The otters liked him, I guess. He was cold too, but not like you."

Gerta rested her chin on a stone at the edge of the pool. There was a pile of clothing near the edge. This led to the realization that she was naked, and so was Janna, and that was...interesting.

"So what did happen?" asked Janna.

Gerta tried to tell her.

It was hard to put words on the experience of the thorn hedge. She was sure that she was doing it badly, and she found herself saying things that were not quite right, but she did not know what the right words would be.

"It was angry because of giving berries to birds?" said Janna, baffled. "Not because she killed the...whatever it was...sorceress... that made it?"

"Not exactly." Gerta sighed. "I don't think death bothered it. But it thought of itself as kind—not that it thought, exactly—but it was doing a kindness, and the birds did one back, and the Snow Queen stopped spring from coming so that the thorns couldn't do that, then the birds couldn't do it back. And that made the thorns very upset."

It sounded ridiculous when she said it out loud, but it had mattered so much when she was in the thorn-dream—the birds, the berries, the gift given and received. "I suppose if you're a plant, that sort of thing is important."

"Huh," said Janna.

She put her arm around Gerta's shoulders, and Gerta found that she was not at all bothered by that. She leaned her head on the bandit girl's chest, and then something else occurred to her.

"Where did the reindeer hide go?"

Janna shook her head. "Gone," she said. "Under the plants and the stone. I pulled it off so the otter could grab you."

It hurt less than Gerta expected. "Well," she said. "Bury it under scree or under earth, Livli said. I don't think it can get any more buried than that."

"I'm sorry," said Janna.

The old reindeer had saved her, had given her a way to think underneath the Snow Queen's gaze. Gerta shook her head. "It's all right," she said. "It was good to be a reindeer, but...I think it would be greedy to want more."

She rested her forehead against Janna's collarbone and breathed the mineral scent of water. She could feel her pulse, or perhaps it was the hoofbeats, far away, of the reindeer road. "I'll miss it," she admitted. "But I don't think it'll go away, either. Not really. I can sort of feel it, in the back of my head. That's how I got out from under what the Snow Queen was doing. The reindeer saved me."

"Us," said Janna. "He saved us."

Gerta smiled up at her, surprised. "Yes," she said, and then Janna bent down and kissed her. Her lips were even warmer than the hot spring and that was all right, too.

Chapter Thirty-Nine

When they put on their clothes at last, and slogged up to the fire, the otters came galloping to greet them. Gerta laughed and nearly staggered as they brushed against her in a wave of fur and whiskers.

"You're fine."

"We knew you would be."

"We said to keep you warm."

"The hot springs are excellent."

"We like them very much."

"They could fix anyone."

"They fixed you."

"The palace has fallen down."

"Herself is gone."

"No, she isn't."

"Yes, she is."

"She's gone enough."

"She's wrapped up in tree roots."

"She's made of winter."

"She won't be free by spring, though."

"Spring will end her."

"Enough!" said Gerta, still laughing. "Thank you! You saved us all."

"It's true."

"We did."

"We are very brave."

"You are very brave and very talented and very wonderful," said Janna. "And you all know it, too."

The otters looked very pleased.

"Is she really gone?" asked Gerta. "Will spring really end her?"

"It will," said Glitter.

"Spring has not been here for a long time," said Glint.

"We are nearly sure of it," said Ur.

Mousebones landed on her shoulder. "Awk!" he said. "Awk-awk! Awk!"

Gerta waited for him to say something coherent. "Hi, Mousebones."

The raven bent forward, meeting her eyes. "Awk! Aurk?"

The first whisper of unease touched Gerta. "I can't understand you," she said.

"Awk! Awk! Awk!"

"He says that the magic fell off you," said Ur. "It was clinging to you like snow to a leaf, but you melted it all off." She sat down and scratched her ear.

"What?" said Gerta, bereft. "It did? You mean I can't understand you any more?"

"Awk," said Mousebones grumpily.

Gerta remembered what Livli had said about magic filling her up like a pot, and then being poured back out again. Or the way Mousebones had described it, like frost on a branch. Had the frost finally melted off?

Perhaps I couldn't have used the reindeer skin any more anyway...

The skin hardly seemed important, compared to Mousebones.

"But you're my friend! I want to talk to you. How can I get the magic back?"

The raven huffed, gaped his beak and said, in a hoarse, creaky voice "You...can't..."

Janna started. "Hey! I understood that!"

"Stupid...human...speech. Awk!" He shook his head, as if to clear it. "Could...go...get some...other magic...maybe. Don't... know...where. Find some...somewhere..."

"Wait a minute," said Janna. "Are you telling me you could speak human all this time? Why *didn't* you?"

"I didn't...feel...like it..." croaked Mousebones. He launched himself off Gerta's shoulder and took to the air.

"I'm gonna wring his feathered neck," said Janna, to no one in particular.

Gerta laughed.

As they reached the fire, though, her good mood faded.

Kay was gazing into the fire. His hands were wrapped in bandages torn from blankets.

He also had the beginnings of a truly magnificent black eye. Gerta tried to feel bad about that.

"Hello, Gerta," he said. "You're awake."

"I am." She crouched down next to him. "How are you feeling?"

"I'm cold. And my hands hurt." He sounded very young.

"I'm sorry," said Gerta.

He was silent for a little while, and then said "I think I'd like to go home."

"Okay."

"He'll be all right," said the other boy. He had pocked skin, and a faint accent she couldn't place. He was also very ugly, which surprised her a little. She thought the Snow Queen only took pretty boys, but his face was badly scarred.

Well, who knows what a spirit of frost finds pretty?

The boy smiled at Gerta encouragingly. There was a gap in his front teeth, oddly familiar, like something she had seen once in a dream. "I'm Shan. Your friend will be all right. The heart thaws more slowly than the rest. It takes time."

"Was your heart not frozen, too?" asked Gerta.

He shook his head. "I went with her willingly—more the fool I—but I tired of the palace quickly. But the otters told me what

209

happened to those who tried to leave. So I did not try. Eventually I think she forgot me, or grew tired of me. I saw a few others come and go, but she froze them when they became restless."

"She was very beautiful," said Kay abruptly.

"Yes," said Shan kindly. "She was."

Kay lifted his head. His eyes passed over Gerta without really seeing her, and it came to Gerta that he had looked over her like that many times before, that his frost-colored eyes had never really seen her.

A year ago, it would have made her frantic, but now it just seemed easier that way.

He said, "The snow's melting. It shouldn't melt. We'll see what's underneath."

"Only temporarily," said Shan. "It'll come back."

Kay relaxed. "That's good, then."

Gerta looked at Shan helplessly. The boy shook his head. "Give it time," he said quietly.

Gerta did not particularly want to give Kay time. It seemed that she had given him quite a few years already, for all the good it had done her. "We'll take him home," she said. "His parents can take care of him."

"You're putting the cart a bit before the horse," said Janna. "How exactly are we getting home, anyway?"

"Oh, that," said Mousebones. The raven landed next to them, preening under his wing.

Shan clapped his hands together. "A raven that talks! Well, I should not be any more surprised than that otters talk." He bowed very deeply to Mousebones.

"Courtesy," said Mousebones. "I...ap...awk! *Approve.*" He glared at Gerta. "Only...for you...would I try to say *P.* Stupid mammal sound."

"You were saying?" said Janna. She leaned over to Gerta. "Finally, I can answer him back when he insults me!"

"I have never insulted you," said Mousebones. "I have merely p…pointed things out in the—sp—awk!—*spirit* of constructive criticism."

"Sure," said Janna. "Now about getting out of here…"

Mousebones flapped past them, around the edge of the fallen thorn hedge. They left Kay in the care of Shan and followed. The otters wove around them.

"How's your ankle?" asked Gerta.

"Better after soaking it. You were out for over a day, incidentally." Gerta blinked.

Mousebones landed on something sticking out of the jumble of snow and dirt at the base of the thorns.

"It's Herself's sled!"

"We know that sled!"

"We can fly if you hitch us to it!"

"Assuming the magic isn't gone."

"It shouldn't be."

"It's our magic, not hers."

"Didn't it used to be Herself's?"

"It's ours now."

"I could fly if I wanted."

"Like a raven."

"But no flapping."

"Flapping is right out."

"Can you dig the sled out?" asked Janna, shouting to be heard over the flow of otterish enthusiasm.

"Of course."

"Obviously."

"Probably."

"Let's find out."

Snow flew. Gerta and Janna fled to a safe distance.

"I didn't imagine we'd fly home," admitted Gerta.

"I didn't imagine any of this," said Janna.

Gerta stood up on her toes and kissed Janna, because she could. It seemed to work just as well as it did when Janna kissed her. She made a mental note to do it as frequently as possible.

Janna grinned down at her.

"Will you come home with me?" asked Gerta plaintively.

"I suppose I have to. Otherwise you'll be home for five minutes and something terribly bizarre will happen to you and when I see you again, you'll have befriended three chickens and a whale."

"Oh, good," said Gerta, folding Janna's hands in hers. "Because I'll have to go home and see my grandmother. And I imagine Shan will want to go home, and we'll have to drop Kay off with his parents."

"Sooner rather than later," muttered Janna.

The largest of the otters—*Fish-eater*, Gerta thought—got the edge of the sled in his teeth and backed up. The others grabbed onto the tangle of traces and pulled too, and it came up out of the snow, beautifully carved, white as snow.

One of the otters slithered up into the harness, moving like a furry snake, and leapt. The sled came up off the ground for a few inches, then settled back down.

"It still works!"

"I knew we could do it!"

In the end, Shan and Janna had to harness up the otters, who kept squirming and slithering over top of each other. The sled came up off the snow three or four times, until Shan cleared his throat and looked beseechingly at the otters and when that didn't work, Janna cursed them out soundly.

"Sorry."

"We get excited."

"Flying is very exciting."

"But not flapping."

"That was a good curse, though."

"It had real venom."

"We will behave."

212

They loaded Kay into the back and Shan took up the reins.

"Are all of us quite ready?" he asked.

Mousebones clenched his feet in Gerta's pack and hunched down, muttering.

The otters sorted themselves out and began to gallop across the snow.

The sled came up off the snow with a shuddery sensation, and then they flew.

Chapter Forty

It was like nothing that Gerta had ever felt before, nor, to be honest, did she want to feel it again. It was magical and terrifying. The otters were slipping and slithering over thin air and surely the magic could give out at any moment. Wind screamed over their heads.

She dug her nails into the carved ivory grips. "How do you do this?" she shouted at Mousebones.

"I fly a lot slower!"

They circled over the top of the mound. A green web of stems held down a pile of rubble larger than Gerta's entire village back home.

"Will the plants die in the snow?" asked Janna in her ear.

Gerta dragged her mind, with difficulty, away from the horrors of flight. "I don't think so. The green stuff will wither under the snow, but the wall was very…very *strong.*" Janna nodded, satisfied.

"I've flown like this before," said Kay thoughtfully. The wind blew his hair back from his face, and his eyes were watering—or possibly he was crying.

The otters turned the sled south and began to gallop.

Everyone ducked down out of the wind. Shan poked his face up over the front, looked at the reins, then shrugged and dropped them. The otters ran through the sky without human direction.

It was a long ride and very cold. Gerta and Janna huddled together for warmth. Janna laughed ruefully. "This is the trip of a lifetime," she said, "and I will be glad when it is over. How did she do it?"

"She must have had magic to keep the wind out," said Gerta.

The sun set over them. The stars came out. Ducked down below the level of the wind, Gerta looked up.

"Look," said Janna, pointing up at the great band of stars. "The Bird's Pathway."

"They don't look any closer," Gerta said.

"They never do," said Mousebones. "And it's a stupid name. You can't fly anywhere near them. Or the moon, either." He sounded disgruntled.

They flew on and on through the stars, which did not get closer, and the moon rose at a great distance away.

When the sled landed on the roof, at first Gerta didn't recognize where they were. The otters pranced and bounced, and one— *Misting,* she thought—said, "This is it, right? The place where we got the last one?"

Gerta stood up unsteadily. Her knees were cramped from so long hunched down in the bottom of the sled. She looked out across the snowy rooftops.

Perhaps it was the angle. Perhaps she had been away too long. For a long moment, she did not know where she was.

But then the familiarity struck her, and the village settled into place like a bone back into the socket. "Oh," she said. "Oh. Kay— we're home."

They had to land in the street and lift him out of the sled. His hands were too badly damaged to climb down on his own.

"Home," he said. "Yes. I would like to go home."

He went up to the doorway. Gerta knocked for him and then stepped back. She slipped her hand in Janna's as they watched.

The door opened. A golden square of light fell out onto the step, and she saw Kay's father in the doorway.

The cry of joy and grief and astonishment was muffled by the snow, but they all saw Kay pulled inside and his father's arms surround him.

Gerta let out a long sigh.

She had done it. It was over.

She thought that she should feel triumph or joy or pride or… something. Mostly, though, she felt tired.

"Is this where you're going?" asked Ur. "We can take you somewhere else."

"Not in that thing," said Janna. "Unless Gerta wants to?"

"No," said Gerta, turning back. "I have to go and see my grandmother. She'll worry. Maybe we'll come and visit you someday."

"We would like that."

"Yes."

"Bring fish."

Shan only nodded. Janna shook his hand and Gerta kissed each of the otters on the nose. "You are marvelous," she told them. "You saved our lives."

"We are very marvelous."

"We are quite excellent otters."

"You brought down Herself."

"We didn't like her very much."

"There was never enough fish."

"Will you be able to get out of the harnesses?" asked Gerta. "Once you've dropped Shan off?" She remembered being a reindeer, and the tightness of the harness and the complicated snaps and baffles.

"Oh, yes."

"Maybe not back in again."

"We could if we wanted to."

"We hardly ever want to."

The otters arranged themselves in a straggling line, still bickering, and galloped into the sky.

And then it was only two girls and a raven, alone in the snowy street.

"We should go in," said Gerta.

"Yes," said Janna, and didn't move.

"My grandmother will be there."

"Yes."

Gerta nodded. She stood up on her toes and kissed the bandit girl and said "We'll go in. And we'll come up with a story about how someone kidnapped Kay and you helped me get him back, which is mostly true, although no one will believe us about the Snow Queen, except my grandmother. And my grandmother will make us tea, and probably there will be a lot of crying and a feast."

Janna nodded. "Tea would be good," she said.

"And after that," said Gerta, "after that, I want to go to the coast with you."

"The coast?" said Janna, sounding surprised.

"You told me about it once," said Gerta. "Where the ravens slid down the roofs in winter."

"I like this idea," said Mousebones. "Will there be sausages?"

"We will work something out," said Gerta firmly. "Because I've never seen the sea."

"Then we will have to fix that," said Janna, holding out her arms, and Gerta settled into them.

"Awk!" said the raven, as they embraced and left no place for a large bird to perch. "Typical. *Awk!*"

Acknowledgments

Hans Christian Andersen was a weird dude.

I know that I am supposed to use the acknowledgments to tell people about everyone who helped with the book, and I'll get to that, but I just want to put that out there first. Hans Christian Andersen. *Wow.*

His idea of a happy ending is that everybody dies attended by angels (or if you are very very fortunate, in church with your feet cut off.) I find his work mawkish, sentimental, and frequently utterly unreadable, and yet there's...something. I can't put my finger on it. (I'm a writer, not a literary critic.) People remember Andersen's stories for a reason. The Snow Queen and the Little Mermaid have joined the popular fairy tale pantheon when other authors of the era are forgotten or obscure. He had a line directly to the lizard brain parts that react to fairy tales. Some people do.

So I suppose my first person to thank is the storyteller himself. I have not the least doubt in the world that he would be utterly horrified at what I have done to the Snow Queen, and yet, I could not have done it without him. Next up, we have the usual suspects—my editor Brooke, with whom I have long, often hilarious arguments in the review comments on the documents and my faithful proofreaders, particularly Cassie Dail who frequently gets drafted as alpha reader these days, and so gets hit coming and going as it were, James Rice, Jes A, and Sigrid Ellis. They are the best sort of people.

This book took a *lot* more research than usual, into things like Sámi culture, Finnish folklore, and reindeer anatomy. A bunch of people helped with bits and pieces of that, but much gratitude to three in particular:

Foxfeather Zenkova, who told me everything I wanted to know about reindeer, including the clacking tendons in their feet and what they smell like.

Heli Kinnunen, a Finnish folklore major and Helpful General Consultant on All Things Finnish. Every tidbit in the book about food, weather, vegetation, neat tidbits of folklore, etc, that I got right is entirely due to her. (Many things are probably still wrong. She says I needed more sauna. She was probably right.)

Niina Siivikko, Finnish-Sámi cultural historian, who went over the bits with Livli with a fine-toothed comb at my request. Anything I got right with regards to accent marks and proper cultural artifacts are due to her kind input.

All three of these people took time out of their busy schedules to share their expertise with me, and I am so very grateful.

My husband, the love of my life, who has to read these books up to five times, whenever I've hit the *oh god this shames my ancestors* point of the writing process. I cannot overstate his contribution. Also, he brings me German chocolate cake when a book is done and I am trying to figure out what to do with my life.

And finally, of course, my readers, of both books and social media, without whom I'd be trying to write books in the spare time between digging ditches and crying into my beer. Thank you, thank you, a thousand times, thank you!

T. Kingfisher
Pittsboro, NC
February 2016

About the Author

T. Kingfisher is a pen-name for the Hugo-Award winning author and illustrator Ursula Vernon.

Ms. Kingfisher lives in North Carolina with her husband, garden, and disobedient pets. Using Scrivener only for e-books, she chisels the bulk of her drafts into the walls of North Carolina's ancient & plentiful ziggurats. She is fond of wombats and sushi, but not in the same way.

You can find links to all these books, new releases, artwork, rambling blog posts, links to podcasts and more information about the author at

www.tkingfisher.com

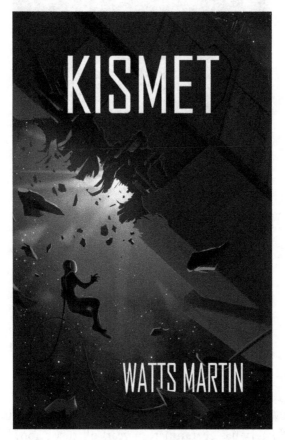

The River: a hodgepodge of arcologies and platforms in a band around Ceres full of dreamers, utopians, corporatists—and transformed humans, from those with simple biomods to the exotic alien xenos and the totemics, remade with animal aspects. Gail Simmons, an itinerant salvor living aboard her ship Kismet, has docked everywhere totemics like her are welcome…and a few places they're not.

But when she's accused of stealing a databox from a mysterious wreck, Gail lands in the crosshairs of corporations, governments and anti-totemic terrorists. Finding the real thieves is the easy part. To get her life back, Gail will have to confront a past she's desperate not to face—and what's at stake may be more than just her future.

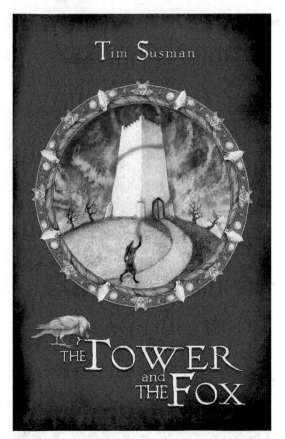

Tim Susman

THE TOWER and THE FOX

For Kip, growing up in shadow of the human men-only Prince George's College of Sorcery has been nineteen years of frustration. Magic comes naturally to him, yet he's not allowed to study sorcery because he's a Calatian—one of a magically created race of animal people. But when a mysterious attack leaves the masters desperate for apprentices, they throw their doors open, giving Kip his chance.

As he fights to prove his worth to the human sorcerers, he encounters other oddities: a voice that speaks only to him, a book that makes people forget he's there, and one of the masters who will only speak to him through a raven. Greater than any of those mysteries or even whether the College's attacker will return to finish the job is the mystery of how Kip and his friends can prove that this place is where they belong…

THE TOWER AND THE FOX BY TIM SUSMAN, $17.95, ISBN 978-1-61450-385-9